T0160291

Weight of Her World

AMANDA OWENS

About the Author

Amanda Owens currently resides in the same small town in Alabama where she was born and raised. She has owned a pet grooming salon for over fifteen years and enjoys getting to spend time with all the dogs that come see her.

Amanda and her wife have been together for fourteen years. They love spending time with their two rescue cats, Roo and Mila, who pretty much run the household, if she's being honest.

Copyright © 2022 by Amanda Owens

Bella Books, Inc.
P.O. Box 10543
Tallahassee, FL 32302

All rights reserved. No part of this book may be reproduced or transmitted in any form or by any means, electronic or mechanical, including photocopying, without permission in writing from the publisher.

This is a work of fiction. Names, characters, businesses, places, events and incidents are either the products of the author's imagination or used in a fictitious manner. Any resemblance to actual persons, living or dead, or actual events is purely coincidental. The publisher does not have any control over and does not assume any responsibility for author or third-party websites or their content.

Printed in the United States of America on acid-free paper.

First Edition - 2022

Editor: Heather Flournoy
Cover Designer: Sheri Halal

ISBN: 978-1-64247-356-8

PUBLISHER'S NOTE

The scanning, uploading, and distribution of this book via the Internet or via any other means without the permission of the publisher is illegal and punishable by law. Please purchase only authorized print or electronic editions, and do not participate in or encourage electronic piracy of copyrighted materials. Your support of the author's rights is appreciated.

Weight of Her World

AMANDA OWENS

BELLA
BOOKS
2022

CHAPTER ONE

"Where are my damn keys, Brynlee?" Mom sits across from me at the dining table. She huffs loudly, clearly wanting my attention. I finish typing the last of my notes before looking up to see the scowl on her face. She is in one of her moods this morning.

"The last I saw them they were on the kitchen counter."

"Well, find them." She bends over to tie the laces on her steel-toed boots. "I'm going to be late for work."

She is always losing her keys. Closing the laptop, I stand to do as I am told. I know to choose my battles wisely with her. I go to the kitchen and scour the counter. There are no keys in sight. I pull open the drawers and rummage through them, moving aside pens, old papers, and lighters, amongst all kinds of other junk. Still no keys.

"Find them?" Mom walks into the kitchen pulling a jacket over her shoulders.

"Not yet. Maybe in your room?"

Mom gives me a hard stare. The crease in her forehead moves down between her brows as they furrow together. "If you do not find those damn keys in the next five minutes you better not ask to drive my car again."

She's treating me like a child while trying to hold yet another thing over my head. It's true, I don't own a car yet. However, I have money in my savings for that. I just haven't gotten around to it. Mom doesn't know how much money I've put back, otherwise I wouldn't have as much as I do. She is always borrowing money from me or asking me to give the boys lunch money for school, which I do without hesitation. I'm already helping with the utilities and groceries. I have to keep some money hidden or I would never be able to get a car. I'm twenty-two years old and still taking the bus everywhere.

I push past Mom to go look in her room, refusing to make eye contact on my way by. She is a tall woman. Her size is threatening to most and I'm no different than anyone else who refuses to confront her. She has a good five inches of height over me.

The keys are on her dresser, hidden behind the picture of Grandma and Grandpa. She probably left them there last night when she came in late. I haven't driven the car in two days. I grab them and jog down the hall, finding Mom in the kitchen pouring coffee into a thermos.

"Here." I lay the keys next to her and back away.

She picks them up along with the thermos and walks toward the door. "I'm working late tonight. Don't forget to pick Ben up from practice." She walks out the door without even a glance backward.

"You're welcome," I say quietly to the closing door. The door creaks back open slightly. My breath catches in my throat.

"Damnit!" Mom shouts as she slams the door shut. "Get some fucking WD-40 and fix this," she calls out.

I release the breath I'm holding as her footsteps fade away. I sink back against the counter, my shoulders slump with relief.

The clock on the microwave practically shouts the time. It's six thirty-five and I still have to get the boys up, feed them breakfast, clean myself up, and get us all to school and work. I've been working at the same place since I graduated high school. Luckily, I found this job early on. This allows me to take my college classes at night so I can help with the boys—the only way to make things work at home. Mom tried to talk me out of college because she needs my help at home. She told me that I can make a good career with the company I am with now and work my way up. But I don't want to spend the rest of my life working in a warehouse.

I climb the stairs to the boys' room, the first one to the right. "Boys, time to rise and shine." I flip on the light, or they will completely ignore me. "Your cereal is on the table. Up and at 'em, you two."

"Five more minutes." Ben rolls over and pulls the cover over his head. His bed is on the left side of the room vertical to the door. Brayden's bed is on the right side next to the doorway. They were bunk beds at first, but we separated them last summer when both boys kept fighting over the top bunk.

"Can't do it, buddy. We are pushing for time."

They slowly move themselves upright in bed. Brayden reaches his arms up high toward the ceiling, stretching as far as his arms can go. He is the youngest of us three at only nine years old. Ben's three years older than Brayden and very mature for his age.

"Okay," Ben says reluctantly, and pushes the covers back to stand. He grabs his T-shirt from the top of the dresser and slips it over his head.

Brayden stumbles sleepy-eyed toward me. He stops in the doorway where I'm standing to look up at me, a big crease across his cheek from his pillow. I rub my hand through his thick brown hair. "You awake, little man?" He bobs his head up and down before wrapping his arms around my waist for a hug. I squeeze him tight and kiss the top of his head.

I watch as the boys descend the stairs, Ben leading the way, then I turn to get myself presentable for the day. My bedroom is just down the hall from the boys. We share the only bathroom upstairs. It's an old house that needs lots of work, but at least it's home.

I take very little time to get ready. I shower after work, so not much time is needed for myself in the mornings. Pulling my long hair into a messy bun, I brush my teeth and quickly dress in my typical work clothes of jeans and a T-shirt.

The boys have finished eating by the time I get back downstairs. I rush them to get dressed and we head out. The school bus stops right in front of the house. It's still lightly raining, but I can see the sun trying to break through the clouds. Brayden stands at my side with his Spider-Man backpack on underneath his blue rain jacket. Ben thinks he is too grown for a backpack, so he's cradling his books inside his black rain jacket to keep them dry. I bought these jackets for the boys a couple months ago for this purpose exactly.

"Are you coming to my practice today?" Ben asks. He is on the basketball team for the middle school.

"Definitely. I'll grab Brayden and we will be right over."

"Is Mom coming?" Ben knows the answer to this question, but it doesn't stop him from asking every time.

I shake my head. "I'm sorry, buddy. She has to work late."

"She's always working." Brayden looks up at me.

"How about we get pizza for dinner tonight?" A change of subject is in order. I would rather the boys start the day off with positive thoughts. They shouldn't worry about why our mother isn't making an effort.

"Yeah!" both boys say at the same time.

The bus pulls up and they eagerly climb aboard to get out of the rain. Ben heads straight to the back to find his friends. I wave to Brayden after he takes his seat. He always looks to see if I'm still waiting.

I walk behind the bus for a bit before it turns left down the next street. My bus stop is two blocks away. The chill of the morning rain makes me shiver underneath my oversized rain jacket. Mom bought mine when I was in middle school and it still fits. She had said she wanted to give me room to grow. And that she did. I could buy a new one now, but I see no reason to when it's still in good shape. There are more pressing things to spend money on.

The bus ride to work is short. I like to walk when it's nice out, but when the weather is like this, I'd rather keep warm and dry. By the time the bus stops to let me off, the rain has ended. Unfortunately, there are still colder days ahead, so the bus and I will be seeing a lot of each other in the coming months.

I step off the bus and the chill of the air hits me. I pull the front of the coat together, closing the gap over my chest. Being in the South, our winter really starts in January and February.

"Hey, B," a familiar voice comes from behind. Andrea and I have been working together since the day I started. We met in orientation and have been friends ever since.

"Good morning." I look down at the cooler in her hand. "What did you bring me for lunch?"

"Sliced Virginia ham and smoked turkey with lettuce, cheese, onion, honey mustard and mayo, on a potato sub with a side of kosher dill pickle, SunChips, and a brownie." The smile of proud achievement spreads across Andrea's face.

"That sounds amazing! I love when you bring me lunch." I bump my shoulder against hers as we walk into work. She had sent me a text last night ordering me not to bring anything today. Her exact words were that she was "giving me the hookup." Andrea is nine years older than me and the only true friend I have.

"Girl, you know I got you."

Our shift starts at eight o'clock. We clock in and begin our fast-paced day in the warehouse of scanning and sorting shipments as they are unloaded from the freight trucks. The job hours are only part time, but it pays so well that it makes up for it. Plus, if we ever want to get extra hours on the weekends, we can. Andrea has a little girl around Brayden's age, so the hours are perfect for her. Being a single mom must be hard. At least Mom has me.

The time goes by fast, and before I know it, the lunch bell rings. We get a short twenty minutes to eat before getting at it again. Andrea is already sitting at our table with the sandwich and chips waiting. I slide onto the seat across from her.

"I'm starving."

"Dig in." Andrea takes a bite of her sandwich and I follow suit.

Immediately, I fall in love with the savory goodness. "This is so delicious." I take another bite before opening the chips. "You're spoiling me."

"It's nice to have someone to share my love for food with. Baby girl has a limited selection of food choices."

"Eight-year-olds and their taste buds."

Andrea smiles. "You've got that right. That child would live off cereal or SpaghettiOs if I'd let her."

"We need to get together soon so little man and baby girl can share a can of SpaghettiOs and you and I can have your famous margaritas."

"Now that's a plan I can get behind."

CHAPTER TWO

It's nice having the house to myself right after work. Though it is only a small amount of time, it's all mine. Now that I am showered and my hair and makeup look appropriate, I can take my time getting dressed. A little music wouldn't hurt with the process.

I grab my phone to select a playlist but stop before I can open the music app. There is a missed call from Brayden's school. How did I not hear that? I quickly dial the number back.

"Hello, I'm Brayden Foster's sister. I have a missed call from the school."

They put me on hold while I'm connected to the principal. This can't be good. His school never calls.

"Hi, this is Ms. Cain, Brayden's teacher. I tried to call your mother, but I couldn't reach her."

"I'm sorry," I say, confused. "I thought I was waiting for the principal?"

"Oh. I apologize for the confusion. I'm the one who called. I happened to be in the office just now when you rang back.

The reason I had called is that I would like to speak with your mother in person about Brayden. Could she meet me today or tomorrow?"

I sit down on the bed. "She's at work, but I'll get her the message." I already know the outcome of that discussion. "Can we go ahead and schedule it for today?"

"Yes. How about after school at three o'clock?"

"That will work." I sigh, knowing Mom will not be at the meeting, though I will ask her. It will be me who goes. I refuse to tell Ms. Cain that bit of info. "Brayden is okay, right?" I'm worried about him now. He's never had trouble at school before.

"Yes, he is. Thank you for returning my call."

We hang up and I immediately dial Mom's work so she can decline. The foreman puts me on hold while he radios Mom to the phone. She will be pissed that I interrupted her. But I have to give her the choice of going.

"Brynlee, this call better be from the emergency room." Mom doesn't disappoint.

"Sorry, Mom, but Brayden's teacher called. She wants to meet with you today at three o'clock."

"What about?"

"She didn't say."

"So, he isn't injured?"

"I don't think so." I want to sigh, but I hold it in.

"Then I'm confused as to why you are calling me. Are you not supposed to handle these things so that I can work and pay our bills? You do like having a roof over your head, don't you?"

I hate when she's condescending. "I just wanted to make sure you didn't want to go. I'll find out what's going on."

"Next time use your brain before calling me at work." She hangs up the phone.

I drop my phone on the bed and feel tears threaten to spill from the corners of my eyes. I quickly wipe them away, not willing to let her get to me like that.

* * *

The halls of the elementary school are quiet before the last bell rings. I've arrived a little early so that I can get Brayden and have him wait for me. I'd rather him not worry about this meeting, but I have no other choice.

I stopped by the office to let them know of my plans. They also gave me instructions to meet Ms. Cain outside her classroom. Now I'm standing in my spot, waiting for the bell to ring. When it finally does, the kids rush out, filling the halls with chatter.

"Brayden," I call out. The kid is on the move. He whips his head around to see who called his name, and when he notices me, the smile spreads wide across his face.

"Bryn!" he says, rushing toward me. His clothes are so cute with his khaki pants, a button-up plaid shirt, and matching brown shoes. His hair is disheveled from the cute little part he had this morning. He has always liked to dress like a little man. That's why I gave him that nickname.

"Hey, little man." I wrap my arms around him as he hugs my waist. He is a small boy. He has never been particularly tall at any age.

"Are we going to Ben's practice now?" He pulls back from the hug and looks up at me.

"Soon," I say. "First I need to talk to your teacher."

"Oh." His tone is restrained now.

"Hey," I say, squeezing his shoulder to get his attention. He looks up at me. "It's just to get an update. I'm sure she is going to tell me what a wonderful student you are. And probably, that you are the most dapper kid in class." I hate seeing the worry on his face. I'm not quite sure why I am here, but he doesn't need to know that.

"Okay," he says. I pull him against my side. "What does dapper mean?"

I laugh. "It means you dress very nice." That gets a smile from him. "Okay, you wait right here for me." I have him sit across the hall from the door. I'd rather he not hear anything said until I know what this is all about. "Maybe you could draw me a picture. I need a new one for my locker at work." He smiles and pulls out his notebook and colored pencils from his backpack.

The door behind me opens. "Hi, Brayden."

"Hey, Ms. Cain. This is my sister."

I stand. "Brynlee," I say, reaching out my hand for her to shake. Her confusion is noticeable as she finally puts her hand in mine. "I'm sorry our mother couldn't be here."

"Nice to meet you." Ms. Cain lets go of my hand. "I'm sorry Ms. Foster was unable to make it." She opens the door to her classroom and motions for me to enter. "Shall we?" I walk past her, getting a faint scent of strawberries.

Ms. Cain leads me to the table in the back of the room. She sits down and offers me the chair across from her. I can't take my eyes off her. I never had a teacher as beautiful as Ms. Cain when I was in school. Her long blond hair is straight and silky. Her big, gorgeous eyes are a deep blue. She looks to be in her late twenties.

"I usually only speak with a parent or guardian of the children." I'm sure she's upset because she was under the impression that Mom would be here.

"I really am sorry. Our mom works long hours and it's hard for her to take time off. I'm the one who usually handles things concerning my brothers. I can assure you that I will tell her everything we discuss."

"Is Brayden's father not in the picture? I couldn't find a contact number for him."

"He is not." Their dad is in jail, but she doesn't need to know that bit of personal information. I try not to let her rattle me. I feel like that question was unnecessary. I understand she is disappointed that mom didn't come, but I am ready to get things moving and find out the reason I'm here. "So is Brayden having trouble in your class?"

Ms. Cain seems to be gathering her thoughts about the situation. She opens a file in front of her. "Brayden's grades have started falling. He seems distracted a lot. And I've noticed he's been sitting alone at lunch and not wanting to pair up for group assignments. I was wondering if there have been any changes in his home life that could be causing this new behavior."

I'm stunned to hear this. Brayden has never had trouble in school, always been an honor roll student. I try to think of anything that could contribute to this behavior. "No. Nothing at home has changed that I can think of."

"Any new people in the house?"

"Not at all." Mom's boyfriend is kind of new, but he doesn't live with us.

"Does he sleep through the night?"

"Yes. Honestly, Brayden is a great kid. He does his homework. He helps out around the house. He's happy. I can't think of anything that has changed. Does he turn in his homework?"

"He does." Ms. Cain shuffles through the file in front of her and pulls out a paper. She slides it over to me. "His homework is always complete and correct. The concern is on his tests. He doesn't finish them."

I take the paper. As I scan over it. I see that on his completed work he has answered almost all the questions correctly. The back of the paper is blank. "Maybe he didn't know there was a back side."

"I make sure everyone knows it's two-sided before handing out the test. And look at this one." She slides another test over. He only answered half the questions and then stopped.

I'm baffled. I look from one test to the other. I see a dog that he had drawn on the bottom corner of both papers. "Does he draw on all his papers?" I'm curious if his doodling is the distraction.

"He does. And it's always a dog."

"Maybe he is just getting distracted by his drawings. He does love to draw." I look up to meet her eyes, hoping this is the answer.

"I don't think that's it, but it wouldn't hurt to have a talk with him about it."

I nod my head in agreement. "I'll try to find out why he isn't interacting with the other kids too." I give Brayden's test papers back to Ms. Cain.

"Thank you for meeting with me today. I hope we can find out the answers to get Brayden back on track. He really is a bright kid and one of my most well-behaved students."

"I hope so too. This isn't like him." I stand, and so does Ms. Cain. "Thank you for calling this to our attention. I'll let you know what we find out."

Ms. Cain smiles. "I would like that," she says, finally seeming to have relaxed. She walks with me to the door, where I grab Brayden from his spot in the hall. He waves goodbye to her as we walk away.

"What did she say?" Brayden looks up at me with hopeful eyes.

"She said you are the most dapper guy in class." He giggles. I hug him against my side.

"Here." He hands me the picture he drew. It's a big yellow dog with a blue collar.

"This is awesome, little man." The smile on his face says it all. I will talk to him about things eventually. Right now, I just want him to be at ease. There is clearly something bothering him that explains the behavioral difference in school, and I need to find out what it is so that it can be fixed.

CHAPTER THREE

After the parent/teacher meeting, Brayden and I went to catch the very end of Ben's basketball practice. Then the boys and I grabbed pizza on the way home. I helped them get settled before leaving for my night class. I'm in my final semester of school so I don't want to miss any classes if I can help it. I hate leaving the boys alone, but I have no choice on some days. They have my cell number, and all the doors are locked.

I arrive at school right before class starts. It's a smaller group with a majority of the students being older. I like it that way.

"Bryn." I hear my name as I enter the room. It's Damon. He and I met on the first day of class.

I walk over and take the seat next to him. "Damon, did you save this seat just for me?"

"Of course. I didn't want you to miss out on sitting next to the smartest guy in class."

I laugh. "Glad you said guy and not person. Because… ahem." I clear my throat dramatically and then smile his way.

"Well, that's a given." He smiles back.

Damon is a nice guy from what I've experienced over the last few weeks. We've sort of become friends. The light banter between us is easy. It doesn't take any effort to get along with him, but because I don't usually get to class early enough, we don't get to talk much.

The rest of class goes by in a blur, and before I know it, we are all gathering our things and heading out of the classroom. My mind was in and out of what was going on in the lecture.

"So," Damon says, stepping up to walk beside me. "How about we swap cell numbers? I wanted to ask you a question about our homework, but I had no way of reaching you."

"Sure," I say. It would be nice to have someone to talk to about the assignments.

"Great!" He pulls his phone from his pocket. "What's your number? I'll text you and then the deed is done."

I give him my number and watch him type out a text. We walk down the hall until we reach the doors and push through to go outside. He looks back down at his phone. "Did you give me the right number?" He laughs awkwardly.

"Oh!" I pull my phone from the bag across my shoulder. "It was still on silent. Yep, here it is." I show him the alert.

"Awesome," he says, spinning around to walk backward down the street. "See you next class."

I wave bye, then take my seat on the bench to wait on the bus. I look at my phone and save his number to my contacts. I also have a message from Ben asking me to bring home some chips and more soda. Those boys are bottomless pits.

* * *

The house is quiet when I get home. I put the bag of snacks on the counter and go in search of the boys. A light is shining into the hallway from their room. I walk softly up the stairs in case they fell asleep watching television.

The door is open. Ben is sitting on his gaming chair playing a video game. He has his headphones on. I assume it's to keep the sound down because Brayden has fallen asleep next to him on his beanbag. He has his thumb in his mouth. I thought he had kicked that habit.

I go and stand beside the television to get Ben's attention and hopefully not scare him in the process. He sees me, pauses the game, and pulls his headphones down around his neck.

"Brayden couldn't hang. Did you bring snacks?" He gives me a big toothy grin. This guy is funny.

"Of course."

"Heck, yeah." He stands and stretches his arms above his head.

"Did Brayden have his bath?" Brayden has on his pajamas, but I still have to make sure. He is only nine, after all, and pajamas can sometimes happen regardless of bath time or not if he is tired.

"Yep. We both did." He walks past me, and I hear his footsteps fade down the stairs.

I pull back the covers on Brayden's bed, then pick him up to carry him over. I remove his socks knowing how hot he gets when he sleeps. I'm the same way. After pulling the covers up, I kiss the top of his forehead. He feels warm. I lay the back of my hand against his head and cheeks that I notice are pink. He feels like he may have a fever. I take off down the hall to the bathroom and return with the forehead thermometer, which I hold to his head. It reads 100.8.

"Oh no." I lay the thermometer on his nightstand, then head downstairs to the kitchen. Ben is putting away the last of the groceries I brought home. He's such a good helper. I pull open the cabinet above the sink and take out the children's Tylenol.

"What's going on?" Ben asks. He is opening the Gatorade I got him instead of the soda.

"Brayden has a fever. Did he seem sick to you tonight? Like any coughing or complaining of a sore throat?"

"Um," Ben says. "Not that I can remember. He was quiet, though. Didn't even ask to play my game." He takes a swig of his drink.

"Okay." I grab a Gatorade and head back up to Brayden. He hasn't moved. I sit on the side of the bed and measure out two teaspoons of Tylenol in the cup it comes with.

"Brayden," I say quietly. He doesn't move. "Brayden." I rub his back. "Wake up, little man." He begins to stir. I run my hand across his forehead and through his hair. He opens his eyes and starts to sit up. I take hold of his arm to help him. "Here." I hand him the Tylenol, then twist the cap off his drink.

He takes a small sip of the Tylenol. "Yuck." He scrunches up his face.

"Swallow it all at once."

He tosses the rest of the medicine back and swallows. I quickly pass him the Gatorade. He drinks greedily.

"How are you feeling?"

"I'm sleepy," he says, handing me the drink and lying back down. "Will you lay with me?"

"Absolutely." He scooches over so I can lie down next to him. He puts his head on my shoulder and his arm over my waist. I run my hand through his hair.

Ben walks in with a bag of chips and his drink. He looks at me and points toward the television, asking permission to keep playing his game. I give him a thumbs-up and mouth the words *thirty minutes*. He nods an agreement.

I lie here not caring about doing any homework or cleaning house. Instead, I just watch Ben play his video game while rubbing Brayden's head until I hear his breathing become deep and steady. I feel so bad for him. He is having a rough time at school and now this. My brain is working overtime trying to figure out what to do to help him.

My eyelids are heavy. Maybe I'll just close them for a moment or two so they can rest a little. When I open them again, after what only feels like a few minutes, it's totally dark in the room. I look around, trying to adjust to the darkness. I search for Ben. He's asleep in his bed. Apparently, I dozed off. Slowly I remove my arm from underneath Brayden's head and walk down the hall to my room. I'm so tired it's all I can do to change clothes and brush my teeth. When I finally crawl into bed, I hug my pillow hoping that tomorrow Brayden will feel much better.

* * *

"What are you doing?" A voice pulls me from my dreams. I open my eyes to see Mom standing in the doorway. "Get your ass up. I'm leaving."

I take my phone off the nightstand to look at the time. Shit! I slept in. How did this happen? I must have forgotten to turn my phone off silent. No wonder the alarm didn't go off. I jump out of bed and rush down the hall to the boys' room. They are not there. I head downstairs to the kitchen. Mom is about to walk out the door for work.

"Where are the boys?"

"Stan took them to breakfast and then to school."

"Why?" I'm confused. They don't like Stan. Plus, Mom never gets them ready for school.

"Because he wants to get to know them better." The sarcasm can't be missed. "If it's any of your business."

"How was Brayden feeling?" I ask, stopping her from trying to walk out again.

"He's fine. Why?"

"He was running a fever last night."

"Okay. Well, he didn't complain." She probably didn't even notice. Stan must have stayed here last night. There's no way he'd make an effort to be here early. "Put some fucking clothes on in case Stan comes back." Mom looks me up and down, then turns to go out the door for work.

I'm wearing my typical sleep clothes—a T-shirt and pair of shorts. It's not in any way inappropriate. But I was rushed thinking the boys were going to be late for the bus. I wasn't worried about changing first, nor was I aware that Stan was here or may come back.

Instead of letting Mom get to me, I make coffee, which I rarely drink, feeling the need for an extra boost of energy this morning. I take my cream-filled drink and head back upstairs to get dressed. There is plenty of laundry and errands to keep me busy. And I haven't even looked at my homework.

Three hours and two loads of laundry later, I'm feeling accomplished. I cleaned the kitchen, living room, bathroom, and showered myself. I go into the boys' room to put their laundry away and decide right then that they will be cleaning their own room today. Ben's stuff is everywhere. It's the complete opposite of Brayden's side of the room. As I'm walking back toward the bathroom to put away the towels, I hear my cell phone ring. I take the towels with me and lay them on the bed.

It's the elementary school again. "Hello?" I answer.

"Hi, is this Brynlee McAdams?"

"Yes."

"I'm the school nurse for Parkland Elementary. I have Brayden in my office complaining of a stomachache, and he has a low-grade fever."

"I'll be right there to get him." I hang up the phone and quickly change into a pair of jeans and a sweatshirt. I slip on my Converse shoes, then redo my hair, making the high bun a little neater with less strands hanging down. I quickly brush on a little makeup and head out.

When I arrive at the school, I'm directed to the nurse's office. But when I walk in, the nurse isn't there. It's Ms. Cain standing next to Brayden.

"Bryn!" Brayden runs to me and puts his arms around my waist as a sob escapes his little body. I squat down, holding him back to see his face.

"What's going on, little man? You aren't feeling well?" He shakes his head and then falls into my body, wrapping his arms around my neck. He has always been a lovey boy, but now I feel like something is going on. I look up to see Ms. Cain watching our interaction.

Ms. Cain walks over to us and puts her hand on Brayden's back, who is still holding tight around my neck. "Brayden," she says softly. "Could you sit in the chair for moment while I talk to your sister in the hall? It won't take long." That last part was more for me than Brayden, as her eyes never left mine.

I pull him from the grip he has around my neck and look into his tear-filled eyes. My heart clenches. "I'll be right back, and we will get out of here. Okay?" He nods. I kiss his forehead as I stand up. He returns to the chair he was in when I entered.

Ms. Cain leads me outside the room and into the hall. She leans her back against the wall opposite from the door. I stand at an angle to her. "I think Brayden may be getting bullied by some boys in class," she says. The look on her face is everything.

I feel like I can't breathe for a moment. "What? Why do you think that?"

"I can't be sure, but I did see a boy bump into Brayden in the hall today, and then another boy come from behind to whisper something in his ear. The look on Brayden's face…" She pauses, and I can tell she is upset. "Did you talk to him last night?"

"No, I didn't have time." Which feels so terribly wrong to say. I should have made time to have that talk. I thought I had a couple days. I never imagined he was getting bullied. "I take night classes for college," I say, feeling the need to explain further.

"What about your mother? Did she speak with him?"

"I didn't get a chance to tell her. We were all asleep when she got home from work last night." It was sort of the truth. Mom tends to hang out with Stan and a group of friends at a bar near their work when they get off for the night. I don't know how she'll take this news, though. That scares me a little.

I see disappointment on Ms. Cain's face. I look down at my hands and study them like they hold the answer to all things in my life. I don't want to look her in the eyes. I never want to let anyone down, especially my sweet and kindhearted little brother. "I'm going to have that talk today," I say. "I will find out what's going on." Ms. Cain lays her hand on my forearm and squeezes gently. I look up at her.

"I know you will. I can tell you're a good sister." She pulls her hand back. I don't know why, but I feel like she truly cares about Brayden and this whole situation. Not because she is his teacher, but because she is a good person.

"Thank you," I say shyly. I turn to go back to Brayden so we can leave. A couple steps forward, though, and I realize a question I didn't ask. My abrupt stop throws Ms. Cain off-balance, and as I turn to face her, she realizes we are about to collide. She pushes her hands forward to brace against the impact and they land on my stomach. I grab her arms to help stabilize her.

"I'm sorry," she says, pulling her hands back. I can almost see the embarrassment.

"No, I'm sorry." I feel my face flush. "I was just going to ask, before we went back in, did you happen to speak to Brayden or the other boys about what you saw?"

"I only spoke to Brayden. I told him what I had witnessed and asked if he wanted to talk to me about anything. He said no. I couldn't get him to open up and I didn't want to push him. I'd rather not bring any attention to the situation with the other boys until we know for sure what is going on. If you could get anything out of Brayden that could help me, then we can take action."

I bob my head as I take in this bit of information. Why is Brayden holding back? Why would anyone bully him? I just can't understand. "Thank you," I say again, because I really mean it.

"One minute," Ms. Cain says, holding up her hand to keep me from turning away. She reaches into her pocket and pulls out a piece of paper, propping it on the wall to write on it. "This is my number. I don't normally give it out, but please feel free to call me if you find out any new information. Or if you just need to talk. I'm here to help." I feel touched by the gesture, but I don't say so. I nod my head and slide the paper into my front pocket.

As I enter the nurse's office again, I see Brayden sitting in the same chair as before, holding his backpack tight to his chest. "Ready to go, little man?" I motion for him to come to me. Brayden looks up and smiles. When I look back toward Ms. Cain, she is smiling too.

"Feel better soon, Brayden. I need my helper back." She squeezes his shoulder as we walk by.

"Bye, Ms. Cain," Brayden says. He looks up at me as we walk down the hall. "She's my favorite teacher."

"I'm glad." I smile. Ms. Cain is kind and beautiful. She'd be a lot of people's favorite.

CHAPTER FOUR

When we walked out of the school it was around lunchtime. I had considered taking Brayden to a med center to get checked out, but not once since we left school has he complained about his stomach. Only that he is hungry. He has mentioned that quite a few times. So now we are sitting at Uncle Ira's Burger Joint. It's the most popular burger place in town. Brayden has ordered a hamburger with only mayo and pickles with fries and a chocolate milkshake. I ordered the exact same, except my burger is loaded.

"How is your belly feeling?" I wonder if his stomach pain is from stress or if he really is coming down with something. The way he ordered his food seems like it isn't the latter. Plus, since we left the school his whole demeanor has changed. He is back to being my happy little brother.

"It's fine now." He shrugs. "Maybe I was hungry."

"Come here." I motion for him to lean forward. I press the back of my hand against his forehead and cheeks. He feels slightly warm, but not hot. "You may still have a small fever. If so, it'll be Tylenol for you when we get home."

"Yuck."

"I know, kiddo."

The waitress brings our chocolate milkshakes and two glasses of water. Brayden immediately digs in to his shake. I've never had to worry about his appetite. That's why I let him order it. He has always eaten well. Both boys do. As skinny as they are, they can certainly put away some food.

I am trying to gauge the right moment to bring up the bullying. I'm afraid to do it before he eats and ruin his appetite. Makes my stomach hurt just thinking of it.

Our burgers and fries arrive, so I decide to wait. Brayden and I take our first bite at the same time. "So good," we say together, and then we both laugh. He's definitely my brother.

"This is exactly what we needed," I say. He nods his agreement and takes another bite. "How about we go get you a new pair of jeans when we leave? Maybe we will get some donut holes from that place in the mall for breakfast in the morning."

"Yes!" Brayden's smile spreads across his face, showing the food in his teeth. I can't help but laugh.

After we finish eating, I pay, and we decide to walk to the mall. It isn't that far away and it's a nice day. I take a deep breath, hoping I'm choosing the right moment to have this conversation and dreading it all the same.

"You know, Brayden, if you ever want to talk to me about anything at all, I'm here for you. Good or bad, I've always got your back."

He nods. "I know."

We walk a little farther. I'm trying to give him the opportunity to open up without having to ask. I'm not sure that's going to happen. "How's school going?" I move a little closer to my objective.

"Fine." His eyes find the road in front of him and stay. His shoulders get stiff and I can see the tension in his face. There is definitely something going on.

"Ms. Cain talked to me about your schoolwork. She said you are a smart guy, but you haven't been finishing your tests." He shrugs his shoulders, eyes still focused on the path ahead.

"Could you please tell me why? I know you better than that. You always finish your work."

Brayden stops walking, covers his eyes with the bend of his arm, and starts crying. I squat in front of him, pulling him into a hug. It doesn't matter that we are in the middle of the sidewalk. I hold him for a minute and let him cry it out. I know he is hurt. I am hurt for him. When I feel the tears ease up, I stand and walk us to the side of a building for privacy. I am going to plead with him to confide in me.

Brayden wipes his nose on his sleeve. "Boys are being mean to me," he says. "They push me around and threaten to beat me up. They told me if I tell anyone they'll make me wish I were dead." His puffy eyes drop a few more tears.

"Do you know why they are being mean to you?" Besides being little jerks, I wish I could say, but refrain. I'm so mad that this is even happening. But I have to think rational. I am the adult here. I must remain calm and get answers so Ms. Cain can help us.

He lifts his shoulders and then drops them in defeat. "They say I'm so dorky they can barely stand to look at me."

"You are not dorky." I look him straight in the eyes. "You are smart, sweet, handsome, and the most well-dressed guy I know. I'd say this even if you weren't my brother."

"They told me if I score higher than them on a test that they would beat me up so bad that my momma wouldn't recognize me." His tears continue to drip from his eyes. "Don't tell Mom and Ben. They'll be mad at me."

"They could never be mad at you," I say, trying to hold my shit together. I feel sick with disgust. Sweat is gathering at my forehead even though it's chilly out. "We are all mad at your bullies. And that's what they are, Brayden. They are bullies. It's not okay to treat other people that way. They're just jealous of you."

"I just want to be normal." His lip quivers with the words. I pull him in for a tight hug and rub his back.

"You are normal. Don't you ever think otherwise." I can't imagine what he's going through, but as his sister, my heart is breaking. "I will take care of this. I promise."

"Okay," he says.

We break away from the embrace. "Let's go get you some new clothes." He nods. "And I think we need a little something extra. Don't you?"

The corner of his lip goes up for a half smile as he wipes his wet eyes.

* * *

"Ben!" Brayden yells, running through the house. "Ben, look at my new haircut!" His footsteps thud loudly as he runs up the stairs toward his bedroom. I place the box of two dozen donut holes on the kitchen counter and follow him up the stairs with my hands full of shopping bags.

"Pretty cool," I hear Ben say. "The girls are going to love it."

"They already do," I say, entering the room. "Tell them about the women at the hair salon, Brayden." Brayden smiles and covers his face with his arm to hide his blush. "The ladies gushed and called him adorable." When I mentioned a haircut to Brayden because his hair was getting long, I didn't expect him to want something different altogether. The women at the salon helped him decide on a style. His hair is cut short on the sides and longer on top with it standing up just enough to give him flair, but easy enough for him to style himself. He's always had good hair.

"You can't get a girlfriend before me, little brother." Ben playfully punches Brayden's arm.

"It isn't my fault they love me." Brayden giggles. His laugh is contagious, so Ben and I join in. "Look at the new stuff Bryn got me." He pulls out two new pair of jeans and four shirts. He holds them up one at a time for Ben to see. "And look." He reaches into the shoebox and pulls out his very first pair of Converse.

"Dude, those are awesome!" Ben takes the shoe to examine it. I can tell he is genuinely happy for him.

"We have stuff for you too." Brayden gives Ben his bags. I love how excited he is, even for Ben to have new things.

"Cool." Ben pulls out his new clothes one at a time. "I love them. Thanks, Bryn." He hugs me.

"You're welcome, buddy. Don't take the tags off in case something doesn't fit. That way we can exchange it." I reach into another bag on the bed and hand him his new shoes.

"No way!" Ben opens the box to his new pair of Vans. "These are so cool!" He immediately tries them on. I knew he'd like them. I've seen him eyeing them for a while now.

"All right, guys, I've got some stuff to do and dinner to figure out. Clean this room up. Okay?"

"Okay," they say in unison.

I walk away to the sound of the boys talking about their new stuff and what they are going to wear to school next. I know what it's like to be that age and not have nice things in school. I never want them to feel that way. I want them to have more than I did. It makes me feel good when they are happy.

* * *

"Where's everyone at?" Mom calls out.

It's eight o'clock and she is just getting home. And it's not from working late. I'm in my room working on the assignment for Monday's class. I close the laptop and go downstairs.

"The boys are playing video games in their room with their headphones on."

Mom takes the plate of food I made her from the fridge to the microwave.

"Something you bought to rot their minds. In my day we played outside."

"Well it's dark outside, so…" I stop mid-sentence, realizing I was being sarcastic. I do not want to piss her off right now. She has had a drink or two and that makes her even more edgy with me.

She turns to look at me but surprisingly doesn't say anything back. She removes her plate from the microwave and carries it into the dining room. I follow and sit across the table from her.

"I had to go to Brayden's school again today." I wait for a reply, but nothing. She never even asked about the meeting yesterday. "The nurse called and said he was running a small fever and he had a stomachache. When I got there his teacher was with him and she asked to speak with me in the hall. She said she thinks Brayden is getting bullied. When I asked him about it today, he—"

"Bullied? Are you fucking kidding me?"

"No. He was upset about it and—"

"Brayden!" Mom yells. She gets up and goes to the bottom of the stairs. "Brayden, come down here." She sits back down and takes another bite of her food.

I'm not quite sure if I should finish telling what happened or not since she didn't seem to mind interrupting me twice.

Brayden comes running down the stairs. "Yeah, Mom?"

Mom rests her fork on the side of her plate and sits back in her chair. "Are kids picking on you in school?"

Brayden immediately glances at me. His face turns white like he's seen a ghost. My heart drops. "Yes, ma'am," he says, his voice weak.

"What are they doing?" Her face is stern.

Brayden repeats everything he told me earlier. He was so brave and didn't cry, though I did see his lip quiver a few times.

"Come here." Mom motions him over to her. He walks over and stands in front of her. "You are going to have to stand up for yourself. Show me how to make a fist."

"Mom, please," I beg.

"Shut up!" She spits the words at me.

"Show me your fists, Brayden." He does as he is told. "Now next time those boys bully you, you take these"—she grabs his fist with her hand—"and punch them right in the nose." Brayden starts to cry. "Dry up those tears. If you don't stand up for yourself now, you'll always let people walk all over you. I won't have it."

"Mom, not everyone is a fighter." I look at Brayden. "You don't have to fight."

Mom's brows furrow. "Are you going to go to school with him and protect him every day? How about in high school, college, and when he gets his first job?"

"We can talk to his principal and teacher. She wants to help put a stop to this."

"No. Then he'll get picked on even more for being a wuss and a tattletale. You are not a wuss, Brayden." She holds him by his shoulders as tears run down his cheeks. "You are my boy, and you will be tough. You will come out on top. You understand?"

"Yes, ma'am." Brayden wipes his eyes.

"Now go have fun." She taps him on the backside as he turns to leave.

Mom turns on me as soon as Brayden is up the stairs. "What the fuck is wrong with you? I say what happens to my kids." She is seething. "So next time you decide to have an opinion, keep it to your damn self!"

"Mom, he isn't tough like that. He's scared. Please just let me talk to his teacher."

"No fucking way. You better stay out of this, and I mean it." She picks up her fork and points it toward me. "And next time you decide to change the boy's hair, you better ask me first."

"Okay." I get up from the table and go back to my room. I'm so frustrated I can barely stand it. I don't want to be in the same house as her. I pick up my phone and text Andrea. *Plans tonight? Drinks?* My homework can wait. I just need to get out of here.

No plans. Come over. I've got a variety of drinks.

On my way, I message back. I feel more like going out, but this will be fine too. Andrea is fun to be around and I enjoy her company. I could use a distraction right now.

CHAPTER FIVE

"I thought you'd never get here." Andrea opens the door before I even reach her front step. "Get in here."

"I have to Uber, remember." I point to my chest. "No car."

"I know. I was just ready for my drinking buddy. I may have started without you." I follow her through the living room and into the kitchen where she hands me a drink.

"What's this?" I ask. The fancy glass holds a green liquid. I'm pretty sure it's a martini. I've just never had one before.

"Green apple martini. It's good. And strong." Andrea's eyes widen as she refills the half-drunk glass next to her.

"Strong is good." I take one sip. It's delicious. I down the rest. In my defense, it wasn't that much.

"Damn, girl." Andrea laughs. "Hard day?"

"Yes." I feel a catch in my throat, but I clear it away. I kind of recap what has happened. Andrea listens, like the good friend that she is, and lets me spill my guts.

"Oh, honey. Come here." She stretches her arms out for me to hug her. I walk into her embrace. The only hugs I ever get are from her and the boys. "I think we need to go out on the town. Baby girl is asleep. Let me call the sitter and we can let loose."

"Are you sure? I don't mind hanging out here. Plus, I didn't really dress to go out."

"I have plenty of clothes. Follow me."

She leads me down the hall of her two-bedroom apartment. We walk past Aimee's room. She is sound asleep with only a Barbie nightlight on. When we get to Andrea's room, I sit on the end of her bed while she calls the lady who sits for her on occasion.

"All set." She drops the phone next to me. "Now let's find something to wear." She looks me up and down as if deciding what to do with me.

"What?" I laugh.

"I love those jeans. The small tears are super cute. Here." She pulls out a long-sleeved black shirt with slits in the shoulders and tosses it to me. "Try this on. And…" She digs in the bottom of the closet. "Yes. These will look great." She brings over a super cute pair of black ankle boots. Good thing we are about the same size.

She goes back to the closet to find herself an outfit. I take off my top and slip on the black shirt, then pull on the boots. I go stand in front of her full-length mirror.

"Yes, girl," Andrea says. "You look fine as hell."

"You're crazy," I say, but I do like how I look. "Can I borrow a little makeup?"

"Of course. In the bathroom." She points down the hall. I do have some makeup on from this morning, but it definitely needs to be touched up and a little more added for nighttime flair.

A few minutes later, Andrea walks in. "What do you think?" She puts her hands on her hips and sways to one side for a dramatic pose and then throws her hip to the other side and poses again.

"Beautiful as always." She really is an attractive woman. Her light brown skin is beautiful along with her chestnut-colored eyes. She is wearing a white scoop-neck sweater with dark jeans and tall boots.

"Says the woman with the killer body and gorgeous green eyes." Andrea shakes her head at me as if she knows the secret that I haven't been let in on. I always feel so ordinary even though Andrea tells me I'm insane for thinking that. She's definitely a confidence builder.

There is a knock at the door. "The sitter," Andrea squeals. "You ready?"

I nod. "Let's go."

* * *

I've never been to this bar before. Andrea heard about it from her cousin Kendra. It's low-key. Bluesy music, low lights, and a mixed variety of people. It's on the south side of town. In other words, the uppity area.

We head over to the bar area where Andrea's cousin and her friends are gathered. She introduces me to everyone. I've never met this group before, only Kendra one other time.

Andrea faces me at the bar. "What you drinking?"

"Um, Jack and Coke?" It comes out more as a question than an answer. I have no idea why.

"For real? After the couple days you had, we deserve something a little different." She bumps my arm with hers.

"Okay, what new drink are we having?" I look at the drink menu in front of us.

"Let's try an old-fashioned. I've never had one, but they look good."

I shrug. "I'm in."

Andrea orders our drinks. The bartender has them to us quickly. "This first one is on me." She taps her glass to mine. "Cheers."

I take a large sip and swallow. Not what I expected, but not bad either. I scan the room. It's a really cool place.

"Let's grab that table." Kendra points to the middle of the room where a group is getting up to leave.

When we get to the table I sit beside Andrea, the other three filling in the remaining seats. I take my phone out to see if I have any messages from the boys. There's none. I scroll through my contacts and stop on Ms. Cain's number. I hit message. I look at the blinking cursor to type a message, but I don't know what to say. Plus, it's too late to message a teacher. And what would Mom do if I went behind her back? I click the screen off and lay my phone down. I'm supposed to be having fun. I need to try that for once.

I take another sip of my drink and realize I drained it. "Another?" I ask Andrea, jiggling the ice in my glass.

"I'm good for now." She laughs.

I make my way back to the bar for another. I stay there for a moment after getting my drink and take in my surroundings. The blues music is catchy. I get why people like it. I have no clue what this song is, but I enjoy it. I also feel those two drinks creeping up on me. I open my eyes, which I didn't even know I had closed, and see a beautiful blonde looking at me. I look closer. I know her. My legs start walking before my brain can stop them.

"Hi," I say, stopping at the end of the round booth against the wall. "How are you, Ms. Cain?"

"Hi, Brynlee. It's just Sarah." She smiles at me. I feel my heart skip a beat. She is even more beautiful than last time I saw her. I don't know how that's possible. "These are my friends, Ginny and Marla."

"Hello." I nod at them.

"We were just going to grab another drink," the one Sarah introduced as Marla says, as she stands up.

Ginny follows. "Yeah, I'm parched." She smiles at me as she walks off.

"Care to sit?" Sarah offers.

"Sure." I slide in next to her, drink in tow.

"I thought I saw you walk in earlier with a woman."

"Yeah, I'm here with my friend Andrea." I search out the table where she is seated and point toward it. "We're up there." When I look back at Sarah, she quickly looks away and in the direction I pointed. Was she just staring at me?

"I come here quite often. I've never seen you in here before. Are you even old enough to drink?" Sarah smiles. She's teasing me, and I like it.

I laugh. "Is that a serious question?"

She turns her head to the side and looks toward the ceiling as if contemplating that question. Her eyes find mine again and the corner of her mouth lifts into a half smile. "Yes. How old are you?"

"Twenty-two." I raise my eyebrow. "And you?"

Now it's her turn to laugh. "Twenty-nine and holding." She looks at me as if just seeing me for the first time and not just as Brayden's sister. "You've never been in here before, have you? I feel like I would have noticed."

I think Sarah may be flirting with me, but I am a little tipsy so I could be just reading into it more than usual. "This is my first time," I admit. I watch as she takes a drink of her martini. It's a clear drink with olives, unlike what I'm having. Then I notice the wedding ring on her hand. Bummer. "I didn't know you were married." I'm not usually so blunt. I better slow down with the drinks.

"Oh," she turns the ring around on her finger and then removes it. "I'm not. This"—she holds the ring up—"is my way of getting people to leave me alone when I'm out and don't want to be bothered." She puts the ring in her pocket. She could have just told me about it and left it on her finger. But she didn't.

"I don't really have that problem." Not that I go out that often. And I can't believe I admitted that to her.

"Now that's hard to believe." Sarah looks at me, her left brow slightly raised, and it is sexy as hell.

I feel the butterflies in my stomach. I can't remember the last time I had those. We stare at each other for a moment. My mind is blank except for the thought of how incredibly beautiful she is.

"How's Brayden?" she asks, bringing me back into the harsh reality of my life.

"Um." I look down at my glass and swirl the amber liquid. "It's complicated." That's the best answer I can give.

"Is everything okay?" she asks. I look up to meet her eyes and she seems genuinely concerned.

I want to tell her everything, but I don't know if that's possible. "Can we talk some other time?" I look into her big blue eyes. Her blond hair is long and straight down past her shoulders. Her lips are tinted pink with lip gloss. It's easy to see why she needs the ring when out. Who wouldn't want to talk to her?

"Of course." Her face is serious now. "You have my number if you want to talk tomorrow."

I nod. "I may take you up on that." I look toward the bar and see Sarah's friends watching us not too subtly. I scoot out of the booth. "I don't want to keep you from your friends."

"It's okay. I'm glad you came over." She pushes a strand of hair behind her right ear, showing off a silver hoop earring. "Have a fun night, Brynlee."

"You too." I turn to go back to Andrea. Marla and Ginny wave at me from the bar. I wave back. They are friendly.

"Hey, B," Andrea says as I sit down next to her. "You get lost?"

"I saw Brayden's teacher and went to say hi."

"Oh, did you tell her what you found out?"

"No. It wasn't the right time. She told me I could call her tomorrow. I have her cell number. Should I?" Andrea has a good head on her shoulders, so I trust her opinion.

"I think you should. If your mom finds out, though, you'll have to be prepared for the backlash." She takes my hand in hers and squeezes it. "You know I've got your back."

"I know. Thank you." I can always count on Andrea.

"Is that Brayden's teacher? The tall blonde in the middle?" Andrea waves her hand in the air as she looks over my shoulder.

I turn around to see Sarah, along with her friends, waving goodbye on their way out. "Yes." I wave back.

"She's gorgeous." Andrea fans herself.

I laugh. "Yep." That is one hundred percent true.

CHAPTER SIX

I open my eyes to the bright rays of sunlight streaming through the window and the smell of bacon. Where am I? I look around. Oh yeah, I'm on Andrea's couch. I hear a television in the background.

"Momma," Aimee whispers loudly, running through the living room and into the kitchen. "Can I have a juice box?"

"Yes," Andrea says. "But, baby, that is not a whisper."

"Hey, she tried," I call out, my voice sounding raspy.

"Well, hello, sleepyhead." Andrea walks into the room. "I thought you were going to sleep the day away."

"What time is it?" I roll onto my side and reach for my phone. "Almost eight o'clock. Are you kidding me?" I furrow my brows at her crazy talk.

"Well, baby girl has been up since six thirty." Andrea's eyes go wide as she puts a hand on the top of Aimee's head. "We've been practicing our indoor voice to let you sleep. I was wondering if the smell of food would wake you."

I sit up on the couch. "You're making breakfast? I could eat a whole pig right now."

Andrea chuckles. "Will bacon and pancakes suffice?" I nod. "Let's eat." She motions me toward the kitchen.

I slowly roll off the couch and carry my phone with me to the table. Andrea hands me a plate with two pancakes and three slices of bacon. "I like this kind of service." Aimee comes over and climbs in the chair next to me. "Hey, kiddo, do I not get a hug?" She giggles and rushes over to wrap her arms around my neck. I squeeze her back before she lets go and jumps in her chair to take a bite of her pancake.

The food looks so good. I take a big bite of bacon. "Yum," I say, closing my eyes and wiggling from side to side. Aimee laughs.

"That's what you call soul-touching food, baby," Andrea tells Aimee.

I nod. "It's true."

I open my messages and see one from Damon asking to meet up today to compare our homework. He sent that last night at eleven. I didn't even see it. There is nothing from the boys. I normally don't stay overnight anywhere, so I'm a little surprised they haven't checked in.

"Are you going to call her today?" Andrea asks. There is no need to say who; we both know who she is talking about. Andrea sits down at the table across from me with her plate of food.

Sarah was actually the first person on my mind before my eyes opened. I think I may have dreamt about her. "I don't know." I look over at Aimee, knowing I need to watch what I say in front of her. "I want to, but…" What? I'm afraid to make my mother mad. That's the only excuse I can think of. I can't say any of this out loud, especially in front of Aimee.

"It would be a good thing. Don't overthink this."

I let out a small sigh. "I know."

I take another bite of the fluffy pancakes and then type out a message to Damon agreeing to meet. I wouldn't mind having lunch in a few hours at the café a few blocks from my house. It has nice big booths suitable for going over homework.

* * *

The back door to the house is locked. That's unusual at this time of day. I don't have a key to this door, so I walk around to the front of the house. I try the handle first. It's locked as well. I pull the key from my pocket and stick it in the keyhole. The door swings open, pulling the key out of my hand and to the ground.

"How nice of you to finally come home," Mom says. She stands in the doorway, arms crossed, blocking it with her body.

I reach down and pick up the key. "I stayed with Andrea last night."

"You didn't think it was responsible to let me know you were staying out all night?" She still hasn't moved to allow me in.

"I'm sorry," I say, a little confused. I didn't think she would care.

"I might have wanted to go out last night, but you were being selfish and only thinking of yourself." And bingo, there it is. The real reason she is pissed.

"Can I come in?" I really need to take a shower. Plus, it is a little weird she's making me stand outside.

"Let's get one thing straight." Mom points her finger at me. "You want to live here rent free, then you will be coming home at a decent time from now on. You have no responsibilities. So, the least you can do is help me with your brothers."

Wow. That's what I really want to say to her. I do more for those boys than she ever has. I carry my own weight here and then some. I always have. I hold my frustration in and give her the answer I know is required of me. "Okay." I keep my face as normal as possible to get through this confrontation.

Mom must be satisfied with my response because she steps aside to let me in. I go straight upstairs. The boys' door is open. I pop in to say hello. I feel bad leaving Brayden last night after what he had to go through, but I needed a little time to myself to regroup.

"Hey, little man." Brayden is sitting on his bed drawing. I go over and sit beside him. "What are you drawing?"

He shrugs. "Nothing much."

It looks like a dinosaur with trees and a river. "That's a great picture." I'm used to him only drawing dogs. This is a change.

He doesn't respond back. I assume he is upset with me for telling Mom about school. I decide to give him his space. I understand his stresses and don't want to push him. I kiss the side of his head and go over to Ben, who is playing a video game, of course. I run my hand through his hair. He looks up at me, pauses his game, and then pulls off his headphones.

"Where were you last night?" he whispers loudly. "Mom was so angry."

"I'm sorry I wasn't here, buddy. Were you and Brayden okay?" I can't believe Mom griped about me not being here. She never spends time with the boys. You would think she would use the weekends to interact with them.

"Yeah, after Stan got here." Ben sticks his finger in his mouth and pretends to gag. "We went to dinner. Stan told lame jokes and I fake laughed. Then he showed Brayden how to box."

"How so?" What the hell is Stan up to?

"He put his hands up like this." Ben lifts his hands up as if saying hi. "Then he had Brayden punch them." Ben takes his right fist and hits the palm of his left hand. "He said he is going to get us some boxing gloves so that Brayden and I can practice."

"What? That's insane. You are so much bigger than he is."

"So?" Brayden speaks up. "That's the best way to learn. Stan says it'll make me tough."

"Brayden you don't have to fight to show how tough you are. Fighting is not the answer." I look back to Ben. "Don't listen to everything Mom and Stan say about fighting. There are ways to handle things without violence."

"I know," Ben says. "I was just telling you what happened last night."

"Thank you." I give him a kiss on his head. "I've got to go get ready to meet a friend for lunch."

"Can we go?" Ben asks. "Stan is coming over and I'd rather not be here. Mom is pushing us to hang out with him. It's annoying."

"I don't know, bud. I have a lot of work to go over with Damon."

"We'll be good," Brayden begs.

I look over at him. He looks hopeful. How can I say no? "Sure. I'm going to leave here at eleven thirty. Be ready to go by then."

"We will," both boys say with excitement.

* * *

The place I picked for lunch is right down the road and has a very cool-looking interior. It's a retro café with black-and-white checkered floors. The booths have turquoise leather seats, as do the tops of the barstools in front of the long counter in front of the kitchen. They also have the best ice cream and milkshakes, which is why the boys love to come. I can't deny it. This place reminds me of the diner in *Back to The Future*.

Damon is already at the café when we get there. He is seated by the window looking at the menu. He doesn't see us walk in.

"Hey, stranger," I say, walking up to the table. He looks up smiling, but that falters momentarily as he sees the boys next to me. I imagine he is confused as to why I brought them with me. "These handsome guys are my brothers Ben and Brayden."

"Hello, fellas. Are you here to protect your sister?" Damon chuckles.

"You better believe it." Ben holds up a fist and shakes it at him.

"Apparently the menu for today includes a knuckle sandwich." I smile to lighten the mood, then push Ben's fist down. Though I know he is only joking, this hit a little too close to home with the whole Brayden situation.

Damon laughs and holds his hands up as if to surrender. "I'm a good guy. I promise." He crosses his heart.

"All right," Ben says. "I guess you're fine. But I am watching you." He moves two fingers from his eyes toward Damon's. He is such a funny kid. He never has trouble meeting new people. Brayden is quiet and a little more reserved, like me.

"The boys are going to be on their very best behavior. They are mainly here for the dessert." Ben and Brayden nod in agreement. "Care if we move to the big booth in the corner? That'll give us extra room."

"Not at all." Damon picks up his books and laptop to stand.

I sit next to Damon with Ben and Brayden to my right. We all order hamburger, fries, and sodas, except for Brayden who gets chicken fingers. Damon and I dig into the web development assignment where we have to come up with an algorithm for the new software design the teacher gave us. I think I have it figured out already, but Damon is double-checking his work with mine.

I take the first bite of my hamburger that the waitress dropped off a few minutes ago. I'm enjoying the juicy goodness when I hear Brayden yell out, "Ms. Cain," whiling waving his hand vigorously in the air.

I look up to see Sarah standing at the entrance. She is looking around trying to figure out who has called her name. When she spots Brayden waving, she smiles and waves back. Sarah makes eye contact with me and begins to walk toward us. I quickly chew my food and swallow, trying not to choke and embarrass myself in the process.

"Well, hello," Sarah says, stopping next to Ben at the end of our booth.

"Hello," I say, pushing down the last remnants of my food. "Funny seeing you here."

"Right?" Sarah smiles. She glances toward Damon then back to me. "My grandmother loves this place. I'm visiting her today, so we ordered takeout for lunch." I wonder if her grandmother lives in my neighborhood.

"The ice cream is good too," Brayden chimes in. I already know he is going to want that for dessert.

"I agree, Brayden. Are you feeling better?" She glances at me briefly. I see her eyebrows rise slightly before letting them fall again. She's probably remembering our conversation last night.

"Yes," Brayden says, then takes a crinkle fry and dips it into the ketchup.

"I'm glad to hear that." Sarah looks over at Ben. "Is this your brother?"

I realize that I rudely have not introduced anyone. "Yes, this is Ben." I point toward him and he smiles close-lipped, thank goodness, because he still busy stuffing his mouth with food. His only focus is eating when food is in front of him. "And this is Damon. We have class together at the university."

"Hi, Damon. I'm Brayden's teacher, Sarah Cain."

Damon reaches out to shake her extended hand. "Hello," he says, finally looking up from the computer.

Sarah looks from me to Damon. "You look like you're working on an assignment together."

"Yeah, it's for our class on Monday," Damon says as he sits up straight to take in Sarah fully. I wondered when he would pay attention to her. She is captivating, wearing tight blue jeans and a long gray cardigan over a white T-shirt with a pair of slip-on shoes. She looks casual and sexy all wrapped up in one.

"What's your major?"

"Software engineer," I answer for us both.

"Wow, good for you two." Sarah stares at me for a moment longer than I would have expected. "I better go grab my order and head out. My grandmother is expecting me any minute. I hope you all enjoy your lunch. Good luck on the assignment."

"Bye, Ms. Cain." Brayden waves.

I watch as she goes to stand in line. "Boys," I say, not quite understanding my thoughts. "Let me scoot out." I motion for them to slide out of the booth. I'm not sure if I have lost my mind or what, but I feel something urging me to go talk to Sarah alone. I'm a little nervous, especially after last night.

As I almost reach Sarah, she steps up to the counter to pay for her order. I quickly turn to go stand by the door to wait for her. It feels a little different now after having seen her outside of her work. When she turns to leave the counter, she spots me standing at the door. The grin on her face causes my stomach to tighten.

"Hi again," Sarah says as she gets close.

"Mind if we talk outside?" I ask, holding the door for her. She nods and walks through the open door. I follow. We stand just to the side of the entrance so as not to block it. "Sorry to bother you. I know you have to get going."

"I don't mind. Everything okay?" She seems confused.

I turn my back more toward the door so the boys can't see my face. "I just thought that maybe you and I could talk tonight. We could grab dinner somewhere?" I raise my shoulders in question. Sarah's expression is neutral, which makes me feel like this was a mistake. "I mean, it's just to talk about Brayden. If you have other plans, that's completely okay." I rush to explain myself so that she doesn't think I'm asking her out. Not that I wouldn't go out with her. I just don't see why she would be interested in me.

Sarah looks down at the bag in her hands. She folds the top of the paper bag over one more time. I can tell she is thinking. I only wish I knew what she was thinking. It sure would make me feel better to know whether it is good or bad. She raises her eyes back up to meet mine, looking a little more relaxed now. She is beautiful. "Yes," she says. "Let's have dinner and talk about Brayden."

"Great." I remain cool, though I want to smile. I had feared I was overstepping by asking her to dinner. But after I explained myself, she relaxed.

"I know a quiet little restaurant down on the Southside where we can talk privately and have a good meal. It's about two blocks from the bar last night. Would that be okay?"

"Yes." The Southside is a good distance for me, but I wouldn't dare say anything. I would take three buses to meet Sarah if I had to. She is going to hopefully help Brayden have a stress-free time at school. That matters more than the travel time. Also, I'm pretty sure I have a crush on Sarah.

"The name of the place is Alfie's. Seven o'clock sound good?"

"I'll meet you there."

Sarah smiles. "I really must be going now." She lifts the bag of food up. "A hungry grandmother is waiting."

"I'm so sorry. Yes, please go." I motion for her to leave. "See you tonight."

Sarah starts to turn. "Bye," she says with a wink. My heart almost jumps clean out of my chest. I put my hand over my heart from pure instinct, not paying attention to my actions. Sarah's eyes follow my hand, amusement on her face.

I immediately turn to go back inside, mortified that she saw me do that. Hopefully, she thinks that I have indigestion or something like that.

I get back to the booth and slide in next to Ben. "Why is your face red?" he asks.

"Must be a windburn," I lie, then look over at Damon. "So, what did you find?" He starts to go over the material. I'm so glad to have the spotlight off me. Now I have to mentally prepare for tonight's dinner and keep my face from being "wind burnt" again.

CHAPTER SEVEN

The Uber driver pulls up to the restaurant in record time. The swerving in and out of traffic wasn't at all what I needed. I thought I could listen to music and relax on the way over. Instead, I spent the whole ride gripping the door and holding on for dear life. I quickly exit the insane car. There really should be a sign on the side of the vehicle saying something like, "I'll get you there fast, no matter the cost." A little double meaning for a heads-up.

The restaurant is remarkably busy. Sarah said it was a quiet place. I guess I assumed it wouldn't be this popular.

"Welcome to Alfie's," the hostess greets me as I enter.

"Thank you. I'm meeting a friend for dinner. I'm not sure if she's here yet. Her name is Sarah Cain." The hostess looks at her book. I am almost fifteen minutes early, which I was not expecting. Ugh, I feel so rattled from the harrowing trip over. I'm not even sure I'll leave him a tip, though the odds are in his favor because I always leave a tip regardless of service or I'll feel guilty. I need to stop thinking about that ride and focus forward.

"She's not here yet, but there is a reservation in her name. If you will follow me, we have your table ready." I was not expecting Sarah to have made a reservation. Good thing for it, though, since Mr. Lunatic Driver got me here quickly.

The Italian restaurant is gorgeous. I had looked it up online earlier to see how to dress. I'm so glad I did. Every table has a white tablecloth with a candle in the middle. The lighting is lower than any place I have ever been. Everyone in here is dressed in business casual attire. I decided to go with my dark-wash jeggings with black booties, a gray blazer over a black dressy tank. It's my go-to outfit when I need to dress up. According to Andrea, it shows all my curves in all the right places and I should flaunt them.

The hostess stops in the back corner of the restaurant away from the crowd. It is a two-person table with no one around close enough to hear our conversation. It's actually perfect. If I didn't know better, I would think this was a date.

I sit down at the table, laying my phone facedown next to the wall. I thought it would be a minute before the server came by, but I didn't have to wait long. A short, dark-haired man steps up to me, dressed in a white shirt with black bow tie and black pants.

"Good evening. My name is Gerald. I'll be talking care of you tonight." He places a menu in front of me and one where Sarah will be seated. "May I start you off with a drink?"

"Um," I say, looking down at the menu trying to find the list of drinks. I definitely need something to help me calm my nerves. "I'll take a Jack and Coke, please."

Gerald rushes off with a smile on his face. I am not a fancy drinker. I'm not really much of a drinker at all, to be honest. But I have found myself leaning more to it for the extra comfort lately.

I look at my phone, but then realize Sarah doesn't have my number and there would be no text from her. I switch it to silent so we don't get interrupted at dinner. I am so nervous about going behind my mother's back. It feels so wrong. I also know that this is the right thing to do because Brayden needs help.

Gerald drops off my drink and promises to return when my dinner companion arrives. His words, not mine. I take a few big swallows of my drink, hoping to ease my nerves. I pull the menu closer and survey it. I have no clue what to order.

"Well, don't you look nice."

I look up to a smiling Sarah standing behind her chair. And wow, she is stunning. She has on a blue fitted V-neck sweater, black jeans, and tall gray boots. Yes, I did let my gaze roam her and I pray she didn't notice.

"Thank you," I say, and smile back at her. I want to return the compliment, but my mind is scattered.

"You're welcome." Sarah takes the seat across from me.

Gerald is on point. Sarah has barely sat when he strolls up to our table and asks for her drink order. He doesn't even give her time to look over the menu. Apparently, there isn't a need anyway as Sarah immediately orders a glass of cabernet.

"What are you drinking?" She gestures to the glass in my hand.

"Jack and Coke." I actually felt like a beer, but this drink seems like it would look a little more interesting. I don't know why I care about appearances. I guess it's because Sarah seems more sophisticated than what I'm used to.

"I'm not much of a whiskey drinker. I prefer wine, when given the choice."

"I've never tried wine before," I confess, and watch as Sarah's brows shoot up in surprise.

"Well, we will—" Sarah's words are cut off by Gerald's wine delivery. He also slides a wooden tray of bread onto the middle of the table along with a small thing of butter.

Sarah leans forward just a tad as if she is going to tell me a secret. "The bread is fantastic here."

"It really is." Gerald nods. "Would you like another drink?"

I look down at my drink when I realize he is talking to me. It's pretty much empty. That went down a little too easy. "Yes, please."

Gerald rushes off again to give us time to look at the menu.

"Have you ever been here before?" Sarah asks, staring at me with those gorgeous blue eyes.

"No. But it seems like a nice place."

"It is. How about we look over the menu and order, then we can dive into our talk about Brayden." Sarah smiles, then lifts her drink as if to take a sip but stops right before it touches her lips. "I think you should try this." She extends the glass of wine toward me. "Everyone should try wine at least once."

I wonder if that's what she was going to say earlier before Gerald interrupted her. "Oh, I'm good with this." I tap my finger to the whiskey glass.

"Are you sure?" She grins and lifts one brow in question. "You might like it."

I can't help but smile along with her. Why do I feel like this has a hidden meaning?

"Sure, why not." I reach out and take the wine from her, allowing our fingers to graze. I look up to see Sarah staring at me, the smile gone. Her eyes seem a darker blue under the lights here. I press the glass to my lips and I take a sip of the red liquid. Sarah's eyes lock on mine and hold. I feel a little self-conscious, but I shake it off and push through. "It's good," I say, handing back the glass.

"Yeah?" Sarah nods and her smile returns. "I know you are young, but I wondered if you would like a red wine." She winks at me to let me know she is only teasing. The butterflies in my stomach flop around.

"Young looking," I say, "but my experiences make up for that." Oh. My. God. Did I just say that? I immediately blush, realizing how my words may have sounded. "I didn't mean it like that." I shake my head. "Just life experiences." Now I do sound young. I should have just left it alone and played it confidently. I look down at my menu and pretend to study it hard in hopes that Sarah doesn't notice my pink cheeks.

Sarah chuckles. I refuse to look up. "Brynlee," she says, and waits for me to look at her. "That was a great comeback regardless of how you meant it."

I prop my chin on my hand to cover at least one side of my face. Sarah is still smiling. It was funny, even if it was an accident. I match Sarah's smile, allowing myself to settle into the moment. Sarah is amused and I did that. I should enjoy it.

"I can make some food suggestions if you'd like. I've been here plenty." Sarah changes the subject though her eyes have never left mine nor her smile faltered.

"Please."

Sarah goes over a few dishes she highly recommends. It's perfect timing too because Gerald makes his way back for our order. Sarah orders first to give me time to think about what I want. She gets some type of seafood carbonara. I decide on the gnocchi alla bava. It has eggplant, ricotta, mozzarella, and parmesan cheese. I've never eaten eggplant before, but I'm not that picky. Gerald rushes off again with our request in tow. He seems like he really enjoys his work. Good for him.

"So, tell me about Brayden." Sarah leans back in her chair, one arm resting on the table with her hand on the stem of her wineglass. She gives me her full attention.

I feel my nerves kick in a little. "Well." I take a breath. "I'm actually going against my mother's wishes by talking to you, but I feel like I have to for Brayden's sake." I reach for my drink, needing a little courage. I don't know what's gotten into me. I look up to see Sarah watching, waiting for me to continue. "You're right. Brayden is getting bullied at school."

"I was afraid of that." Sarah nods her head slowly. Her eyes move down to the table and then back up to me again. She seems concerned—I can tell by the furrow in her brow. "How are you going against your mother's wishes? Does she not want me to help?"

"She believes it's a sign of weakness. She wants Brayden to stand up for himself."

"But he shouldn't have to alone."

"Trust me, I know. I've said as much, but I was told to mind my own business, which is hard to do when I've been the one practically raising the boys." I stop talking, stunned that I just confessed that to her. I am usually a private person. "I'm sorry. It's just a lot."

Sarah's face softens as she leans forward to prop her arms on the table. "You don't have to apologize to me. I can tell you care for your brothers. That's why we're talking now—because you want to protect Brayden. You're doing the right thing."

"Thank you." I release a sigh of relief. It's nice to have confirmation. "I'm afraid that Brayden and this boy, or boys, are going to fight. That's what he is being taught to do. I need your help."

Sarah reaches out and places her hand over the top of mine. "We'll figure something out together." I look down at the contact. My heart seems to thump a little harder against my chest. Sarah makes me feel a lot of things. And one of those is trust. That's not something I'm used to. She pulls her hand back to her side, causing my eyes to follow. "I'm going to need to tell the principal," she says. "We need to address this with the parents."

"No." I sit up straighter. "We need another way. If my mom finds out, then shit will hit the fan. Excuse my language, but it's the truth."

"Okay." Sarah nods as if trying to understand my dilemma. She reaches up to hold her chin between her forefinger and thumb while looking off to the side. I watch her deep in thought while my mind is scanning how beautiful she is in this moment. Her straight hair is framing her face. Her long lashes are painted with mascara, eye shadow brushed across her lids, and lip gloss tinting her lips. She has a little more makeup on than I do, although she doesn't need it.

"I'll have to handle this myself." She looks back toward me with a sense of determination. "That's the only way I know to do this. Your mother can't say anything if I intervene while something is happening. I'll keep a close eye on Brayden. The only problem is that I am not with him every step of the day. But I promise you to try my best. Maybe in the meantime you can try to talk your mom into coming to the school and speaking with the principal. I would feel more comfortable handling this the correct way."

"I'll try my best to get her to come around. But she is pretty adamant on her stance."

"If I can catch the boys in the act, which isn't the best scenario for Brayden, it can help solve the problem. We all will go to the office and parents are called." Sarah pauses. "Would your mom come to the school for that, or would it be you?"

"More than likely it would be me. Mom doesn't like to be bothered at work unless it's an emergency."

Sarah leans back in her chair and takes a drink of her wine, which is getting low now. "I consider this to be pretty important. Don't you?"

"Of course, I do. But my mom and I think differently. Last time I called her at work regarding the meeting you asked for, she said, and I quote, 'You'd better be calling from the emergency room.'"

Sarah purses her lips at that revelation. I have no wish to make my mother look bad in front of someone else. I'm just trying to let Sarah know how Mom is so she can fully understand the position I'm in.

"Mom is good to the boys. Don't get me wrong." I want to give her some credit. She does have a good side. "She is just very tough and wants them to be tough as well."

"Is she a good mom to you?" Sarah surprises me with that question. I've never had someone ask me that before.

"She—"

"Ladies," Gerald says as he approaches our table, cutting off what I was about to say. And I am happy for that interruption because I didn't know how to answer. He has a tray with two plates lifted shoulder high in one hand and a bottle of wine in the other. "Dinner is served." He sets the bottle on the table before placing our plates in front of us. He asks Sarah if she'd like a refill of wine. She nods her confirmation.

"Bon appétit," Sarah says, a smile spreading across her face.

We dig into our food. "This is delicious," I tell Sarah.

"I love that dish." Sarah points at my plate with her fork. "It's one of my favorites."

"You have good taste."

"I've been told that before." Sarah winks and my stomach flips. I don't recall anyone ever winking at me before, and Sarah is making a habit out of it, causing me to react every single time.

We eat our meal with only occasional light talk. It is a comfortable feeling not having to push too hard for conversation. As I finish eating, feeling satisfied, I look up to see a tall, incredibly attractive woman walking toward us. She is wearing a pantsuit with heels. Her hair is super short, but very stylish. She makes eyes contact with me, almost sassy-like, and stops at our table next to Sarah. She places a hand on Sarah's shoulder, causing her to look up to see who it is. The look on Sarah's face is one of recognition with a little bit of something else. Her smile falters.

"Hi there, gorgeous," the woman says to Sarah. "I didn't expect to run into you tonight." Sarah's face is speaking volumes right now.

"Reagan, hi." Sarah smiles, but it isn't the same smile I've experienced throughout the evening. "This is a surprise. I thought you didn't come here anymore." Sarah seems as if she is posing this as a question, but Reagan ignores it as she squeezes Sarah's shoulder lightly and looks over at me.

"And who is your dinner date?" The curiosity in her words let me know this woman is someone close to Sarah, or maybe used to be.

Sarah looks over at me and I can almost feel the anxiety radiating off her. "This is Brynlee."

"Hi, I'm Reagan." She reaches across the table with an outstretched hand. Her other hand never leaves Sarah's shoulder. "I didn't expect to be replaced by someone so much younger."

Whoa! Was not expecting that.

Sarah stands so that she is face-to-face with Reagan. "A word, please." She walks away, leaving Reagan to follow.

I do not turn around to see where they go. It's really none of my business, though I do like this new information about Sarah. Maybe I was on the right track about Sarah flirting with me.

"I'm so sorry," Sarah says, returning to her seat and sounding a little breathless. She picks up her wine and takes a sizable drink. "I guess I owe you an explanation."

"No, you don't." I shake my head. I mean, I want to know who Reagan is, but she doesn't owe me anything.

"Reagan is my ex-girlfriend. We broke up a few months ago. Rather, I broke it off a few months ago. She is obviously still…" Sarah lifts her left hand up to the side of her face and gently shakes her head in frustration. Her eyes are closed.

I reach out and pull her hand down to the table and hold it, which is very unlike me. She opens her eyes. "I understand," I say, squeezing her hand for emphasis before pulling away.

Sarah takes a noticeable breath and releases it. "Thank you for saying that. I shouldn't let her fluster me. She was being tacky because we didn't end on good terms."

"I think she was a little jealous to see you with me."

"She definitely was." Sarah relaxes her shoulders.

"I believe she was sizing me up on her walk over. She thought I was the competition." I smile.

"There is no competition," Sarah says plainly, her eyes staring into mine. I feel my insides squeeze. Why did I say that? Of course Sarah wouldn't find that funny. I look down at my empty drink, wishing there were more of it. "Not many would stand a chance against you," Sarah says.

Those words hit me straight to my core, as unexpected as they are. "I don't know about that." I'm not good with compliments, and Sarah seems to be full of them, surprising me every time.

"I do," Sarah says. She looks sincere. Her eyes hold mine for the longest moment. I force myself to look away with the intensity being too much.

"Thank you for coming out tonight," I say, keeping my eyes lowered, too afraid of my own feelings and also not quite understanding them. Sarah has a magnetic pull, and it's strong. "I really do appreciate your help and understanding. I see why you're Brayden's favorite teacher." I look up and smile so that she knows my words are true.

"I'm glad to help. Brayden is a sweet kid."

Gerald brings us our check. I try to pay for Sarah's dinner since I'm the one who invited her out, but she refuses.

I follow Sarah through the restaurant and out the door. When we get to the edge of the curb, she turns to me. "Where are you parked?"

Ugh. I hate not having a car. It's embarrassing. I pull my phone from my back pocket. "Uber is my ride." I click open the app.

"Where do you live? I can drive you." Sarah stands in front of me, her purse over her shoulder and keys in her hand.

"It's okay. Really. But thank you."

"Nonsense," Sarah insists. "My car is right there. Let me give you a ride." She motions with her head toward her car.

I want to say no again, but how can I? She is too damn beautiful, and I find myself willing to say yes to anything she wants from me. "Sure." I shrug.

Sarah leads us to her four-door Honda accord. The graphite color is shiny under the streetlight, as if it has just been washed. The windows are tinted which accentuates its sportiness. She clicks the keypad to unlock the doors. I'm fairly sure this is a brand-new model. I slide onto the dark leather seats. It's sleek looking. This makes me want a vehicle more than ever.

"I love your car."

Sarah starts the engine. "Thanks. Me too. I just bought her about three months ago." She pulls out onto the street. "Do you mind putting your address into the GPS?"

"Could you drop me off at the retro café?"

She looks over at me, confused. "You don't want me to take you home?"

I don't want to lie to her. "There'll be questions if I'm seen with you. It's best to keep things between us for now. If that's okay." I can only imagine what Mom would say if she found out I spoke with Sarah.

"Gotcha. The café it is," Sarah says. I can't tell if this bothers her or not. But I'm hoping she understands.

We listen to music on the drive. She is almost as quick as the Uber driver. Just a little more responsible. I catch glimpses of her when I can, trying not to be noticeable. Her left arm is propped on the door next to the window, and she is running her hand through her hair. She is totally focused on the road and maybe a little zoned out in a world of her own.

"Are you okay?" I wonder if she is thinking about Reagan.

Sarah drops her hand back to the steering wheel and glances over at me. "Yeah." She sighs. "I was just lost in thought."

It is no time at all, and we are pulling up in front of the café. That felt way too quick. I hate that our night is over.

"Thank you for the ride." I put my hand on the door. As I am about to pull the handle to get out, I feel Sarah's hand on my arm. I turn to look at her.

"Do me a favor?" Sarah props her forearm on the middle console. She looks me in the eyes. "Be confident." With those words comes seriousness and compassion. I'm not sure how she means it, but the air is the car feels heavy.

I nod, then open the door to get out. Before I close it behind me, I bend down to look at Sarah. "If it were only that simple. Talk to you soon." I shut the door and walk away. I don't look back at her, though every ounce of me wants to.

CHAPTER EIGHT

Beep. Beep. Beep. The sound of the scanner, as I run the bright red line over the bar code of each box, provides a rhythm of sorts. I like to keep a certain pace as I work so that I don't fall behind. This rhythmic force keeps me on pace and my mind focused. I'm on the third truck this morning and time is flying by. I like being in my own world at work. Focused and efficient. I scan the box, push it down the conveyor, scan the next box, and push it down again. A cycle of consistency. Then the boxes stop. I look up to see people walking away. I glance at the clock on the wall. Lunchtime. I put my scanner in its charging station by the door, then head off toward the break room. I haven't seen Andrea all morning. She's been working in the back office with returns.

I pull four dollars from the pocket of my jeans and stop at the vending machine. Andrea is already sitting at our usual spot with her display of food laid out. I sit across the table from her.

"Is that your lunch?" she asks, eyeing my Dr Pepper and bag of Doritos.

"Yes." I pop the top on my soda and take a drink. "I didn't have time to pack a lunch." I don't tell her Mom and I had an argument this morning which pushed me out the door quickly. Plus, I'm not really in a place to relive that conversation just yet.

"What am I going to do with you?" Andrea pulls apart the already sliced sub and pushes half of it over to me.

"I promise, I'm okay." I slide it back to her. "I'm not that hungry."

"Well, humor me, then." She pushes the sub back toward me. I start to protest again, but she holds up her hand to halt my actions. "I know you aren't trying to hurt my feelings, so I'm gonna let this slide. Now eat that sub and say thank you, bestie." She cocks her head to the side and smiles in that serious but playful manner.

"If you insist." I take a big bite in a dramatic fashion. Just for emphasis, you know. But it's so good, I take another bite immediately before even swallowing the first one.

"I thought you wasn't hungry." Andrea laughs. "Now after you finish that sub in about two seconds, you are going to tell me what's going on. I don't want any ifs, ands, or buts about it." Andrea takes a bite of her own sub followed by a potato chip. "Also," she says between chews. "How can you ever deny my food?"

"I plead insanity," I say, and then smile. Andrea is right—she makes the best food. I just hate feeling like I'm taking advantage of her. She is too good to me sometimes.

"Okay," Andrea says. "Spill it." We have about five minutes to spare before heading back to work. "Tell me what's going on. And don't say nothing, because I know better."

I'm not really in the mood to talk about anything. I just want to mindlessly scan boxes until it's time to leave. "It's just school stuff with Brayden. Mom is being Mom. And I'm juggling all things in my life."

"Damn. I know you have a lot on your plate. But look, you know I'm here for whatever you need. Even if it's just to vent." And I know Andrea means it.

"Thanks. I think after class tonight I'm going to shower and go straight to bed."

"Yes, ma'am. A little R and R can do us all some good." Andrea clasps her hands together on the table and furrows her brows in that serious look I've gotten to know over time. "If you need me, at any time of the day or night, for whatever reason, you call or text me. Even if it's just for dinner, my special margaritas, or a place to hang your hat. I got you."

"I know you do." I smile to lighten the mood. "How'd I get so lucky to have you as my best friend?"

Andrea raises her hands in the air, and says, "The gods rained down upon you." She lowers her wiggling fingers as if they are rain. "And said, you shall have the bestest bestie in all the lands."

We both laugh. Everybody needs an Andrea in their life.

* * *

"You're early," Damon says as I sit next to him. He has his book open and appears to be going over his already finished work. That's Damon.

"Yeah, I didn't have anything to do after work today." Usually I pick the boys up from school, but Mom had Stan do it today. Our argument this morning was all about Stan. The boys didn't want him to pick them up, they wanted me. So, Mom got pissed off and blamed me for the boys not liking him. I have no clue how she came to that conclusion. I've always been nice to Stan. I'm tired of her blaming me for things I didn't do.

"Well, it's nice to talk with you before class starts."

I nod. "How was your weekend?" Anything to take my mind off my troubles. I didn't hear from Sarah today, so I assume all is well with Brayden. I didn't get to see the boys after school as usual because Stan took them to a hockey game. They have never even watched the sport.

"Pretty low-key. I went to hear a friend of mine play a gig on Saturday night."

"Oh, really. Does he sing?"

"No. She plays the drums."

"Ohh...she. That's badass."

Damon laughs. "Why? Because my friend's a girl who plays drums?"

"Of course," I say automatically and with a flair just for fun.

"At least you're honest." Damon seems amused. He hasn't taken his eyes off me. He's acting different.

"That I am." I match his smile. "Seems pretty empty in here today." I look around. Only two people have come in since I did.

"It does." Damon surveys the room. "But most people aren't fifteen minutes early like us. Usually they rush in last minute." He laughs. "Sound familiar?"

"I'm not always last minute."

"But you are." He chuckles. "Every. Single. Time."

"Oh," I say, realizing that's not a good trait to have. That kind of brings me down, and I'm already in a low place today.

"Hey." Damon lowers his head to catch my eyes. "I'm just teasing you."

"It's okay. It's true." I shrug. "I have two little boys I look after most days. So, it's hard for me to be early for anything. But I am right on time."

"You're a good sister," Damon says, and I can tell he is trying to cheer me up again. "Could you adopt me?" He wiggles his brows.

"Dork." I shove his shoulder. Damon is more playful with me than usual.

"You should come out with me sometime. To hear my friend's band, that is. I think you would like them."

"Yeah." I nod. "That might be fun."

"Might be?" Damon raises his brows and tilts his head in a bewildered way. "I'm pretty sure it will be fun."

I smile. "You're probably right."

"Probably?" He gives me that same look. "I'm pretty sure I am right."

I smile. "Okay, okay. You kind of have a point." Now I'm just teasing him back because it's funny.

"Kind of?" Damon says, and we both laugh out loud, drawing other people's attention.

"Just holler at me next time you go," I say.

"How about I text you instead?"

I laugh again. "You're on a roll, huh?"

"Like a pair of dice." He lifts his shoulders in a smirky type of way.

"No, Damon. Just no." And we both laugh again.

The teacher walks in and the room becomes quiet. I'm thankful now that I was able to get here early. I feel more relaxed and eager for class tonight. I graduate this spring, then things will be so much better moving forward. That should be enough to keep me focused.

CHAPTER NINE

Friday morning started off like every other day this week. The only difference is that after the boys got on the school bus, I didn't have to go into work. Some guy that occasionally works on the scan line with me asked if I'd switch shifts. So, I'm off today but I have to work in the morning. I don't mind being off except that Stan stayed over last night and is still here. He apparently doesn't have to be at work until later today. He is sitting at the table drinking coffee and looking at something on his cell phone.

"Brynlee," Stan says, laying his phone down beside his coffee mug. "Come sit and talk with me."

I'm in the middle of cleaning the kitchen and I'd rather not "sit and talk" right now. I have nothing against Stan, per se. I just don't have any interest in getting to know him. Mom has made it hard to want to.

"I won't bite." He taps the chair next to him.

I almost roll my eyes. I go over and sit, but not in the chair he tapped on. I sit on the other side of that chair. Space is good.

He nods, accepting my distance. "I'd like to clear the air between us. I get the feeling you don't care much for me. I'm not sure what I've done, but I'd like for us to start fresh. If that's possible." He smiles. "What do you say?"

"I have no ill-will toward you, Stan. We're good." I smile back at him, but it's forced, and I think he can tell.

"Well, I know if you and I get along, then the boys will give me more of a chance. Your mom says they trust you and will follow your lead."

Mom has never said of any of those things to me. I didn't even know she thought it. The boys do look up to me because I'm the one who takes care of them and comforts them.

I shrug. "I can promise you that I've never said anything bad about you to them."

"What about me teaching Brayden to stand up for himself?" He leans back in his chair and crosses his legs. He is such a complete opposite from my mom. Stan is smaller than Mom in all ways. He is a plumber and has his own business, but still I don't see the attraction.

"You mean to fight. What about it?"

"Brayden said you told him he didn't have to fight?"

"That's not exactly how things went, but okay, you're right. I don't think Brayden should have to fight his bullies at school when he has adults in his life who can help."

"But see, I'm only doing what your mother asks of me. Plus, Brayden does need to stand up for himself."

I nod. "Okay," I say dryly. I have no intention of arguing with him.

"Brynlee, we are all on the same side here. I know what Brayden is going through. I was picked on as a kid until I stood up for myself."

"And did it stop?" I really want to know the answer.

"It did. I got my ass whooped the first few times, but then it stopped because the boys saw that I would stand up for myself. They didn't want to keep fighting me, so instead"—he smirks—"we became friends. They started calling me Stan The Man from that point on."

"Brayden shouldn't have to get his *ass whooped* to prove a point. He has all of us to be there for him. Stan," I say, hoping he will hear the pleading in my voice, "let's stop this before it begins. He's not a fighter."

Stan rubs the stubble on his chin. He seems to be contemplating what I said. "Well, Brynlee." He leans forward and props his elbows on his knees. "I have to stick with my instincts on this one. My past experiences taught me more than having my mother go to the school and stand up for me. It's molded me into the man I am today. I think your mother and I have this under control. It would mean a lot to us to have you on our side. I know you love your brothers. We do too. And together, as a unit, we can have these boys tough as nails."

I stare at him, unsure of what to say. Maybe Mom has more in common with this guy than I thought. "I guess we will have to agree to disagree." I stand to walk away.

"Please don't push your mom on this." Stan stops me in my tracks. "Her temper is quick."

Is he for real? He's been with her for four months. I've lived with her my entire life. I know she has a quick temper. I turn to look him in the eyes. "Stan, you seem like a nice guy, but you should know that I will never stop fighting for my brothers. I didn't have someone to do that for me. I refuse to let them down." I don't wait to hear his reply. I walk up the stairs as quickly as possible and into my bedroom, closing the door behind me.

How dare Stan try to tell me what to do? His advice is bullshit! He is just a steppingstone on Mom's path to the next man. I cannot stay in this house with him downstairs. Andrea is at work. I could hang out with Damon. But, no. I think I'll just go be alone somewhere. Anywhere but here.

* * *

Belle's Beans and Books is a quiet little two-story place. When you walk in it smells wonderfully of brewed coffee, pastries, and books. Maybe the book part is all me, but I feel like it's there.

The bottom part of the café has tables in the middle of the room and a bar-like counter that runs all along the walls with hookups for laptops. The front window has the same waist-high bar that looks outside to enjoy the city. Straight ahead of the entrance is the counter where you order. The bathrooms are to the right of that, and a spiral staircase to the left that leads upstairs. The second level is where all the books and cozy couches are located. If you stand at the rail up there you can see out over the whole lobby of the café. The floor-to-ceiling windows give off a natural light to the place. This has always been my favorite place to unwind.

As soon as I arrive, I order a vanilla cappuccino. The barista writes down my name, where I'll be sitting, and then I'm on my way to relax. And, boy, do I need it.

I usually browse the books, find one I like, and then chill. But today I'm going to catch up on my classwork while listening to music. I head over to my favorite unwinding spot that I occupied as a teenager. Luckily, it's vacant. It's a big brown leather chair situated right beside the railing on the opposite end of the stairs. I sit down in the oversized comfy chair and it brings back memories. I haven't been here in a long time. I've missed it.

I remove the laptop bag from my shoulder and place it on the ottoman in front of me. I leave the table to the right open for my drink. I look through the spindles, out over the lobby, and into the streets of the city. The sun is shining through the windows creating a sunbeam across the room that looks a little bit like a spotlight. It's nice to have the sunrise from that side in the morning. I like to think it gives everyone a beautiful start to the day.

The laptop is thin and small. I remove it from the bag between my legs. I push back into the chair and prop my feet up on the ottoman. I close my eyes for a second, take in a deep breath and allow the air to fill my lungs, then release it slowly.

"Brynlee?" a friendly sounding voice says. I open my eyes. The barista spots me as soon as I look her way. "Here you go," she says, placing the mug on the table beside me. "Enjoy."

"Thank you." I smile at her retreating figure. They aren't busy at this moment. It's early, so most people are at school or work.

The first taste of cappuccino almost touches my soul. This is a much-needed drink. I stretch back out in the chair to enjoy my warm white mug of tasty goodness.

"Hi, there," a voice from behind me says, causing me to jump and almost spill my drink. "Don't I know you?" I look at the dark-haired woman and try to place her. "You're a friend of Sarah's, right?" she says. "I'm—"

"Ginny," I finish for her.

"That's right." She smiles.

"I remember you were at the club with Sarah and, I believe, Marla?"

"Good memory." Ginny seems impressed. "I saw you come up and thought you looked familiar."

I smile. "It's nice to see you again. That was a fun night, huh?" I would love to ask tons of questions about that night. Like if Sarah mentioned me after I walked away.

"It was. We try to go out once a month or so. Sarah hasn't been out much since the breakup. Her ex was a real piece of work. I heard you met her."

Oh. Sarah *has* mentioned me to her friends. I bite back the smile trying to ease across my face. I needed something good today, and this is pretty damn great.

"Yeah. She was…" I try to think of a polite word for the rude woman.

"A bitch." Ginny laughs.

I laugh with her. "I was going to say bold."

"That's a nice way of putting it. I don't know how Sarah ended up with someone like that. She has the biggest heart and is the sweetest person I know."

"I can see that about Sarah. My little brother loves her."

"She was meant to be a teacher."

"I agree."

"Well, I'll let you get back to it." Ginny backs away. "It was nice to see you again. Sarah says good things about you." Ginny throws a hand up as she turns. "Bye, Brynlee."

"Bye." I wave. She remembers my name. Or, maybe she heard the barista earlier. I choose the former as truth.

I push back in my chair again, mug in hand, and take in that bit of information. She said Sarah says good things about me. I wish I knew what those things were. I wonder how I came up to Ginny and what explanation she gave her for us being out together. That feeling of excitement turns slightly toward anxiety. Surely, she wouldn't give out personal information that I shared with her in confidence? I'm probably overthinking the situation. I have a bad habit of doing that.

I pull my headphones from my bag and put one in my ear. I click on my playlist titled *relax* and let the music do its job. My laptop boots up fast, being that it's less than a year old. As I start to type, one of my favorite Colbie Caillat songs plays. I catch Ginny out of the corner of my eye leaving with another woman. They both look my way and smile. Ginny waves and I lift my hand in acknowledgment.

I bury myself in my assignment, not paying attention to the time or anyone around me. I email my work to Damon because he and I critique each other on the big assignments. As I hit send on the laptop, my phone starts ringing. I look at the screen. It's Brayden's school. My heart sinks.

I pull out the earpiece and swipe right on my cell. "Hello."

"Hi, this is Parkland Elementary School. I'm trying to get in contact with Brenda Foster."

"She's at work. Is everything okay?" My heart is thudding in my chest.

"We've had an incident with Brayden. We need Mrs. Foster to come to the school. The principal needs to speak with her in person. He must be picked up from the office today. Are you able to get in contact with her?"

"I'll call now."

As I click the end button, I look at the time. Two fifteen. I hurry and call Mom, praying she'll not short circuit on me bothering her. If she would just answer her cell phone, I wouldn't have to call her work.

First an administrative person answers and transfers my call. Then a foreman answers and puts me on hold. Finally, I hear the phone rattle and I know it's going to be her.

"Yeah," Mom says, sounding out of breath.

"It's Bryn. The school called and needs you there right now to talk to the principal about Brayden."

She huffs into the phone. "I suppose they didn't tell you what's going on?"

"No, but he also has to be picked up by you. I imagine he had trouble with the bullies again."

"Fine. I'll go straight from work."

"How long will that be? I'll call to let them know when to expect you."

"Brynlee, calm down. I'll get there when I get there, and they'll have to deal with it," she utters as if disgusted by me.

"Do you want me to meet you there?"

"No. Get Ben from school and go home."

"Okay."

"Okay," Mom says, then hangs up the phone.

I'm disappointed not to be the one to go get Brayden. My anxiety has my stomach in knots. It's hard to not know what's going on. My way of dealing with things is completely opposite from Mom's. She doesn't want me to interfere with her plans. All I can think about is Brayden. Did he get in a fight? Is he hurt? Is he scared? It will be hard to wait to find out those answers.

CHAPTER TEN

"I wonder if Brayden socked those boys in the nose?" Ben punches the air with his fist.

We are walking down 19th Street headed home. I was at the school early so I could grab him before boarding the bus. He didn't have practice today so he would have been looking for Brayden. He's been taught not to let the bus leave without his brother unless we tell him otherwise.

"I hope there wasn't any nose socking between anyone." All this new interest in fighting comes from Mom and Stan. I hate it.

"Well, it's better to punch than be punched." Ben shrugs his shoulders.

"Only if he is standing up for himself. I certainly don't want Brayden getting beat up." I stop walking and touch Ben's arm, so he stops too. "I hope you understand where I'm coming from. I love you both with all my heart and I only want what's best for you. If someone hits you, then I expect you to take up for yourself. But I'd rather you not fight if you don't have to.

Using your fists is not the answer. I would hope we could find other ways first."

Ben nods. "I know, Bryn. I just wish that I could tell those boys to stop what they're doing to Brayden. But then that would make me a bully."

I pull Ben into a hug, proud of the kid he his. He wraps his arms around my waist. He is almost as tall as I am at twelve years old. It's hard to believe how fast he's growing.

"You're a smart guy. You know that?" I kiss the side of his head and let go of the embrace.

"I get it from you," he says. He usually doesn't get too sentimental, but when he does it means so much because I know he chooses those moments to let me in.

I put my arm around his shoulders, holding him against my side as we start walking again.

"I have a game on Monday at four," he says. "You'll come, right?"

I look over at him. "I wouldn't miss it."

He smiles. "Think Mom and Brayden will be home when we get there?" We are halfway home at this point, and I have wondered the same thing.

"Unlikely. I'm sure they'll be a little later. Should we stop by and grab pizza for dinner?"

"Mojo's?" Ben says, clearly excited by the idea.

"They have the best."

"Let's do it! Maybe it'll cheer Brayden up. Especially if we get the cinnamon bites. He loves those."

"That's a great idea." It makes me happy to know that Ben cares about comforting Brayden.

By the time we arrive at Mojo's, get the pizza and cinnamon bites, thirty minutes has passed. That explains how Mom and Brayden have beaten us home. The car is parked in the driveway instead of the carport for some reason.

"We have dinner!" Ben announces as we enter the house. I place the boxes on the table. I look over at Ben, who seems to be thinking the same thing I am. Where are they? The house is quiet with no one in sight. "I'll look upstairs," he says.

"I'll check out back." I walk to the back door and pull the curtain to the side. Nothing. I go to Mom's bedroom to see if she is there, but all I see is an unmade bed with clothes strewn around the room.

Ben's footsteps are loud as he hurries down the stairs. "Not up there," he says, as he reaches the bottom. We both stand in the living room looking around.

"Weird." I feel my anxiety rise.

"Want to call Mom?" Ben seems concerned too.

I look at my watch. It seems like more than enough time for them to be home. "Yeah, I guess so." I pull my phone from my back pocket. As I'm scrolling over to find Mom's number, the kitchen door opens. Ben runs ahead and I follow closely.

Stan is the first to enter, then Mom, and Brayden last. No wonder her car was already here. Why she took Stan with her is beyond me.

"What happened?" Ben asks, taking the words right from my mouth. He looks from Mom to Brayden.

I finally get a good look at Brayden as he steps out from behind Mom. His cheek is red and looks to have a small cut on his lip. My heart sinks.

"Brayden stood up to his bullies today." Mom ruffles the top of his hair. His eyes never leave the ground. "He's a little roughed up, but he'll bounce back."

Stan is standing silently next to Mom. He is looking at me. Ben turns to look at me as well. I feel my heart rate speed up, and before I know it my feet are carrying me over to Brayden. I squat down in front of him and brush his hair back from his forehead. He looks at me and starts crying. I pull him into a hug.

"It's going to be okay," I say, for him as much for me. He is sobbing, his arms wrapped tight around my neck, his face buried in my shoulder.

"Of course, it's going to be okay," Mom says sarcastically. She looks uncomfortable standing there staring down at us.

I give her my best go-to-hell look. The first time I have ever done that.

Mom shifts her stance, putting her hand on Brayden. "Now stop that crying. This is the time to be strong." Mom keeps her eyes on me. "Stop making him into a pussy. You can't coddle him every time something like this happens."

I ignore her. "Brayden," I push him back so I can see his tear-streaked face, "are you okay, little man? Are you hurting anywhere?"

He nods his head.

"He's fine," Mom scoffs. "Boys, go get cleaned up for dinner." She gives Brayden a tap on his back, but he doesn't budge. She looks at me again. "Stan and I are going out. After the day I've had, I need a drink or two." She turns to leave. "We will be late," she says, without even a glance backward. Stan closes the door behind them.

As soon as she leaves, I turn my attention back to Brayden. "Ben and I got your favorite pizza and cinnamon bites from Mojo's. Let's go upstairs and clean you up. Okay?" I wipe his face, feeling hurt down to my soul. I want nothing more than to take his pain away.

He nods again. He hasn't said one word yet.

"I'll go with you." Ben puts his arm around Brayden's shoulder and leads him away. I follow.

We walk into the boys' bedroom and Brayden sits on the bed. He looks drained. Ben gets him a clean shirt from the drawer, but I see that he is dirty all over and the shirt he is wearing has blood on it.

"How about you jump in the shower real fast and wash off? Then we can eat." I pick him up and carry him to the bathroom. He holds me tight around the neck and buries his head. I realize he is nine years old, but I don't care in this moment. He is my baby brother and I want him to know I will protect him. I haven't done a very good job at it recently, but that will change.

I sit Brayden on the toilet and start his shower. He starts taking off his clothes. "I'll be back as soon as you're out and clean up your cut." He only nods.

I walk down the hall to Ben. He's sitting on his bed. "Will you get Brayden some comfy clothes and take to the bathroom, so he'll have them when he gets out of the shower?"

"Yeah," he says, his head lowered.

"Hey," I say, pulling his eyes toward me. "Everything will be okay."

"I know." He nods, then gets up and goes over to Brayden's dresser.

I go downstairs and turn the stove on warm and place the pizza and cinnamon sticks in there. I hear Ben go to the bathroom and then a few minutes later the shower shut off. I give him a few minutes to towel off, then make my way back to him.

Brayden has his pants on and is pulling his shirt over his head when I walk in. I guide him to the toilet and have him sit. I take a washcloth and run it under warm water and wring the excess. While he did shower, he didn't wash his cut well. It's probably tender.

Ben comes in with us and props against the doorframe to watch. Neither of us has asked for the details. We can tell he is traumatized. Our cheerfully energetic little brother has been broken.

I dab the washcloth against his lips getting the blood off. He flinches. "I'm sorry, little man." His cut is small, so most of the blood must be from his nose. I see traces of blood inside his nostril. After I get him cleaned up, I wash my hands.

"Let's go eat, boys."

Ben pulls Brayden up and they walk out together. I follow behind, proud of Ben for being attentive to his brother.

It's dark in the kitchen now. I flip on the light, then pull the food out of the oven. "Hey, guys, I have an idea. Since Mom is gone for a while, let's eat in the living room." I pull three plates from the cabinet. "Ben could you grab us all a drink from the fridge? And Brayden, you get the napkins." I grab the food and the lead the way. Mom has a strict rule for no eating in the living room, even though I'm the one who cleans the house. But she isn't here right now, so who cares?

"Do you guys want to rent a movie?"

"Sure," Ben says. "We've been wanting to see that Dolittle movie, where the guy talks to animals."

Brayden perks up at that. Ben knows he loves animals. And I know Ben would never choose that movie willingly. He's being sweet.

"Is that what you want to watch, Brayden?"

He nods his head and I see a hint of a smile.

"Sounds good to me." I skip through the channels and find the movie. I sit on the right side of the couch, Ben on the left, and Brayden is on the floor between us at the coffee table. He has a slice of pizza already on his plate.

I get a slice for myself and take a bite. It is the first thing I've had to eat since breakfast. I devour it pretty fast and get another. After my third and final piece, I pull my legs up under me and rest my head against the back of the couch. Brayden climbs up beside me, leaving no space between my thigh and his. He leans into my side, pulling my arm around him. I snuggle him close while we watch the movie. These are the things our mom should be doing with him. But instead she is out getting drunk with Stan and her friends. Her mothering skills are lacking thoroughly. Brayden is not a fighter; he is small and gentle. He doesn't like confrontation. Maybe her approach with the bullies would have been okay with Ben—though I still wouldn't agree—but she is way off with Brayden.

The movie is about halfway through when I feel Brayden slump against me. He is fast asleep. I look over at Ben. He is playing a game on his phone.

"Ben," I whisper. "Run up and pull the bedsheets back." He gets up and quietly climbs the stairs. I scoop Brayden up and carry him to bed.

"Think he'll be okay?" Ben asks as he turns out the lights on our way back to the living room.

"Yeah, he's a tough kid." I don't want to be negative even though I'm worried.

"He hasn't talked at all," Ben says, and I hear the concern in his voice.

"I know. He needs time, I think." I plop back onto the couch with Ben and pick up my phone. There is a text message from

Sarah. It came in an hour ago. I didn't hear any notifications. I open the message.

Brynlee, this is Sarah Cain. I got your number from the school office. I wanted to check on Brayden. And you as well.

I'm a little surprised she reached out to me. *Hi, Sarah*, I begin typing. *He is trying to cope with everything in his own way. As for me, well…I'm heartbroken.* Send.

"Texting your secret lover?" Ben says, and then pretends to make out with his hand.

"What would you know about a secret lover?" I laugh at his silliness. "It's Brayden's teacher. She's just checking on him." And me, but he doesn't need to know that part.

My cell phone rings. It's Sarah. She is full of surprises.

"Is that her?" Ben asks, trying to look at my screen.

"Yes." I stand, holding the phone to my chest, and give Ben The Look. He laughs. I walk out to the front stoop, closing the door behind me. "Hi," I answer the call.

"Hi," Sarah says back. "I thought I'd call. I hope that's okay."

"Of course."

"I wasn't around when the fight started," she says, "but I got there as quick as possible. I'm sorry I couldn't prevent it. How is his face? I feel so bad."

"It could be worse. I just hate that it happened." I sigh.

"I know. I'm so sorry." Sarah pauses briefly. "I met your mother."

"I'm sorry," I say, only half joking.

Sarah chuckles. "You look nothing alike."

"Nope." I take in a deep breath and ask the question burning a hole in my mind. "Would you mind giving me the details of what happened? I've been left in the dark."

"Oh, sure. Yeah." I can imagine she is nodding her head while saying this. "I heard a commotion in the hall between classes and went to check it out. When I reached the boys, they were next to the lockers. Brayden was on the ground trying to get up. He had already been punched once by a boy named Adam. Right before I could get to them, I yelled for them to stop, but another boy named Jackson hit Brayden and knocked him back down. I was just too far away, so they ignored me. From what was said in the office, Adam and Jackson claim that Brayden swung first. Brayden didn't give his side of the story."

"He didn't say anything?"

"I'm afraid not."

I feel like those three slices of pizza aren't sitting well in my stomach. It's rumbling. I get up to pace the path in front of the house in hopes to settle it down. "He hasn't said anything since he got home either. Like, not a single word."

"Your mother didn't tell you what happened?"

"No. She took off right after she brought Brayden home. I cleaned him up, fed him dinner, and we watched a movie. He didn't make it through the whole thing. He was exhausted."

"I'm sure. He's been through a lot today."

I continue my path up and down the walkway, take a detour around the tree in the front yard, then back to the stoop. "I've been thinking." I pause to try to gather my thoughts. "Could we talk in person about this? I mean, would that be okay with you? I can't let him go through this again." I hear a beep in my ear.

"Yes." Sarah's voice is interrupted by the beep again. I look at the screen. It's Mom.

"Tomorrow?" I say. Sarah starts to answer, but I quickly correct myself. "Wait. I'm sorry." I'm trying to hurry so I can answer Mom's call. "It's Saturday. You probably have plans." The phone beeps again.

"It's okay. I—"

"I'm sorry, Sarah," I interrupt. "I really have to get this call. I'll call you back." I swipe over to answer the call before Mom gives birth to a baby goat. I hate that I cut Sarah off and ended the call so soon, especially since she reached out to me and has been so understanding.

"Hello."

"What the hell took so long?" Mom has clearly had a few drinks. "Stan had to go help a damn friend with a water leak. Come get me."

The last thing I want is to be around her while she's drunk. Or for her to be drunk around the boys.

"Did you hear me?" She speaks louder.

"Where are you?"

"Bubba's," she slurs. "Call when you get here. I'm gonna have another while I wait."

"Sure." I hang up. That's exactly what I want to hear. Now I have to go tell Ben what's going on, leaving out a few details.

* * *

I've been sitting outside Bubba's for ten minutes now. I've called Mom six times. She will not answer her phone. I'd rather not have to go in and get her. This place is packed tonight. All of Mom's work friends hang out here. A matter of fact, it's where she met Stan.

Just as I decide that I have no other option but to go in and get her, she comes wobbling out the front door. She's looking around searching for me. "Over here." I exaggerate and wave flagrantly to get her attention. Finally, she spots me and begins to clumsily make her way over.

Mom opens the door and practically falls into her seat. "Took you long enough." She slams the door shut.

I put the car in reverse. Her attempt at an argument will not work because I will not fall into her trap. Though, I know, she'll have more to say before we get home. She's in that mood. Never fails when she drinks. I pull onto the highway hoping that the next five miles will go by fast. I turn the radio on, and Mom turns it right back off.

"You know," she slurs. "I've been thinking. I am sick and tired of you undermining me with the boys. I'm their damn mother. I say what happens, how it happens, and when it happens. You need to get on board with it or get the fuck out of my house."

Whoa! I whip my head toward her so that I can see her face. She is staring a hole in me. I've taken my fair share of crap from her, almost daily, but she has never threatened me like this before. "You want to throw me out because I don't agree with you on the fighting?"

"Did you not hear a damn word I just said?" I feel her shift in her seat. "You don't have a fucking say in how I raise my boys." Apparently, she feels the need to let me know who's the boss. Like I could ever forget.

"Okay, Mom." I don't want to argue with her.

"And start treating Stan with some damn respect. He's asked me to marry him and I said yes."

"You what?" I glance at her.

"You have a hearing problem tonight? We're getting married."

I shake my head. "You barely know him."

"Did I ask for your opinion? What do you know about relationships? Nothing! That's what."

"I know enough, Mom. I just worry. Your track record hasn't been that great."

Smack! The blow to the back of my head forces me forward.

"What the hell?" I grab the back of my head.

"Don't talk to me like that," Mom almost spits. "Have some damn respect. I've sacrificed for you and what do I get for it? Disrespect."

I don't say anything back to her. How dare she hit me? I'm not a child anymore. I drive the rest of the way home as fast as possible. She says nothing else to me because thankfully Stan calls.

I pull into the driveway, turn off the car, and quickly exit. The house is dark. I leave it that way. I head upstairs, letting Mom fend for her own drunk-ass self. I check in on the boys. Ben is playing video games with his headphones on. Brayden is still asleep. I turn and head to my room, leaving the light off when I enter. With the door closed and locked, I find the end of the bed and sit. The back of my neck feels weird from the jolt forward. I massage it gently, only stopping to swipe away the tears that creep out the corners of my eyes. I hate that I allow her to hurt me.

CHAPTER ELEVEN

Work was a welcomed distraction. Now as I clock out at two o'clock Saturday afternoon with a seven-hour shift under my belt, I feel dread creeping in with the thought of going home. I didn't see anyone when I left for work this morning. I'm sure Mom was sleeping off her hangover next to Stan The Man. His truck was parked in the driveway blocking the car. I usually get to take the car on the weekends if I ever have to work. Today I walked, needing the chill of the air to help me deal with the day.

As I step outside into the bright day, I slide on my sunglasses and find a seat to wait for the bus. I'm in no rush to get home. My cell has three messages: two from Damon asking if I want to go see his friend's band tonight, and one from Andrea wanting to get dinner and drinks. While Damon's offer sounds fun, I'd rather be with my best friend.

Yes! I text Andrea back. *Whatever you want to do is fine, as long as I can get a drink.*

Hell yeah, girl! Andrea responds back almost immediately. *Be at my house by six.*

I click off the screen just as the bus arrives. I am a little bit rejuvenated knowing that I don't have to worry about being home tonight. Instead of getting on the bus, I walk down the street to shop. I don't usually spend money on myself, but I feel like something new to wear tonight.

It is two hours later when I finally walk out the last store carrying two bags. I have a new pair of shoes, skinny jeans, and two new shirts. I'm kind of proud of myself. I have just enough time to get home and shower and get to Andrea's. I grab an Uber, and in no time I'm standing in front of the house. Stan is still here.

The front door is closer to the stairs, so I go in there and hope to not run into Mom. When I walk in, I can hear her and Stan in the bedroom talking. I rush up to my room and close the door.

Knock, knock, knock. "Bryn?" It's Brayden. I literally just closed the door.

I swing the door back open. "Hey, little man." I'm so happy he's talking again that I instantly smile.

"I was worried about you." He comes in for a hug.

"What for? You know I had to work this morning."

"Mom was mad when you didn't come home after work. She wouldn't let me or Ben call you."

"I'm sorry." I pull him into my room and close the door. "I went shopping for some new clothes after work." I take my clothes out of the bag and take the tags off. Brayden climbs onto the bed and sits cross-legged. "How are you feeling today?" His cheek is going to have a bruise. The cut on his lip is slightly red.

He shrugs his shoulders.

"I really wish you would talk to me about what happened. I know it's hard. I understand you have a lot going on inside here." I ruffle the top of his hair. He smiles. "But I will always stick up for you." I tilt his head upward so that he is looking at me. "You trusted me, and I let you down. I'm so sorry. I promise not to do that again. You are not alone, and you do not have to fight anyone again. Okay?"

He falls forward and puts his arms around my waist. I kiss the top of his head.

"I need to shower, little man."

"Are you leaving again?" Brayden looks upset. I've noticed he's gotten clingier with me since the fight.

"I'm going out with Andrea tonight. I won't be out too late. You and I can lounge and watch movies tomorrow. I'll even let you choose the movies."

"Okay." Brayden gets up and walks out the door with his head hung low. I feel guilty for having made plans.

I grab my stuff and head to the shower. I make excellent time getting cleaned up. The new clothes make me feel like a new person. I buckle the black closed-toe wedges around my ankle, then grab my phone, credit card, and license.

I poke my head in to say bye to the boys. "See you later, guys."

Ben whistles. Brayden looks heartbroken. I try not to let it get to me. I need this night for myself.

"Where are you going?" Mom asks from behind me right before I walk out the door.

"Meeting Andrea for dinner. I won't be late."

"What if I wanted to go out tonight?" She crosses her arms. Stan is on the couch with his bare feet propped up on the coffee table. Doesn't look like they have plans.

"You went out last night, so I thought—"

"Oh really. I couldn't possibly go out two nights, huh? Thanks for checking in to see if I needed you to stay with the boys. It's not that I give you a place to live or anything."

"I'm sorry, Mom." I really just want to leave and not do this right now.

"Whatever." She throws her hand up and walks away.

I hurry out as quickly as possible to avoid any more confrontation. I don't know why she has it out for me lately. I've never been her favorite, I know that, but she seems more on edge.

* * *

"Damn! You are smokin' hot." Andrea steps back to look me up and down. "You are gonna turn some heads tonight."

"You look good too." I'm standing outside the door with Andrea still inside. "We ready?"

"As we will ever be." She starts to close the door behind her, but Aimee squeals and pushes through to give me a hug.

"Thank you." I put my arm around her shoulders to hug her back. "I needed that."

Aimee looks up. "Bye," she says, then runs away as quick as she arrived.

"She loves you." Andrea shakes her head. "Shy as hell, but just had to get that hug in."

We walk toward Andrea's four-door Mazda. "Aw. I love her too. She's a sweet kid." I look over the top of the car at her. "How'd you get so lucky?"

"Hell if I know." Andrea crosses her eyes at me before sliding into the driver's seat. She unlocks my door. "Praise Jesus for it, because my momma had her hands full with me."

"No!" I laugh, shutting my car door. "Not you."

Andrea backs out of the driveway. "Easy." She chuckles. "You know I got a tender heart." She always says things like that to me. I do believe she wears her heart on her sleeve.

The bar and grill Andrea chose is near the restaurant where I met Sarah for dinner. We've been here one other time before and the food was rather good with a large variety of cocktails.

"Welcome to Sambuca. Do you have a reservation?" I look over at Andrea because I have no idea.

"No, but I called ahead, and someone said they'd put us on the list. Andrea Beckett." She leans forward a little to look at the hostess book. I grab her arm and pull her back. "Just helping." She flashes me a smile.

"Stop." I suppress a laugh.

Andrea loops her arm through mine. "I've got to lighten you up some tonight." She's only joking, but it is true. I need to relax. I've been so stressed lately.

"Give us about five minutes, ma'am, and we'll have your table ready."

"Ma'am?" Andrea turns her head to the side like a dog hearing a strange noise. "Do I look that old?" she whispers, her hand resting on her chest. "Oh lord, if they don't card me for alcohol tonight, just dig a hole and bury me."

I laugh, pulling her to the side to get out of other people's way. "They are just being polite. Also…" I pause, trying not to laugh. "They probably think I'm your daughter."

"Oh, hell no." Andrea pulls her arm from mine. "You've crushed me." I try to loop our arms again, but she pulls away. "Nope. You cannot have my love no more."

"I'm sorry." I'm laughing now. "Please forgive me."

"Brynlee?" a voice from behind me says. I turn, still smiling.

"Sarah." I'm shocked to see her standing in front of me. "Hi." I never called her back. I meant to, but… "This is my friend Andrea," I say, moving my mind past its thoughts.

"Hi." Andrea shakes Sarah's hand. "Brayden's teacher…from the jazz club, right?"

Sarah smiles. "That's me." Her blue eyes find mine again. She is stunning. Her hair is pulled up with a couple loose pieces around her face. She is wearing straight-legged jeans with heels, and her baby blue shirt makes her eyes bright as ever. "I saw you and wanted to come say hello. I'm here with my friends." She nods her head toward the dining area. When I look around her, I see Marla and Ginny watching us. They wave. I wave back. Then Andrea waves, because that's who she is.

"I'm sorry I didn't call you back," I say, and then feel awkward for saying it.

"I'm going to the bar and get us a drink." Andrea lightly squeezes my forearm as she walks away. I'm glad for the privacy. I haven't told her about Brayden—or Mom—yet.

"It's okay." Sarah fidgets with her hands. "I know you've got a lot going on."

"I had to go pick up my mom from somewhere last night," I explain. "Then I crashed when I got back home." I honestly didn't feel like talking to anyone after what happened in the car.

"I understand." Sarah smiles softly to let me know she means it. "Promise." I like that she threw that last part in. "How are things at home?"

"Brayden is talking again. Thank goodness. And I still would like if you and I could talk privately again." I'm hopeful she is still on board.

"You say when."

"Tomorrow?" I lift my shoulders in question. She smiles. "Oh, you eat with your grandma on Sundays, right?" I remember from the café.

"I do." She arches her brow and smiles as if impressed I remembered. "But not every weekend. I'm available tomorrow evening. Want to come to my house for dinner around seven? That way we can talk without interruption. Don't want any more exes interrupting us. Could be yours next time," she says, lightening the mood.

"I don't see that happening twice." I smile. "But I'd love to." I feel a nervous excitement. I'm not quite sure what is happening, but I am just going to go with it.

"Spaghetti or kabobs?"

"I'll eat whatever. I'm not picky. But you don't have to cook for me, I could eat beforehand." And just like that, I stop going with the flow. Me and my overactive brain.

"Brynlee." Sarah smiles. "When someone offers to cook your dinner, you accept. Especially if they can cook the way I can." She winks at me, and I feel myself heat.

"You're completely right. Thank you."

"I better get back. I'll message you my address."

"Tell Ginny and Marla I said hello." I watch her walk away.

Andrea comes up beside me and hands me a Jack and Coke. "You are too obvious. Turn and look at me right now." I do as I'm told. She's drinking a martini. "You've got it bad for her. And I don't blame you. That woman is fine." She takes the olive from her drink and pops it in her mouth.

"I do not have it bad. I just like her."

"Mm-hmm," Andrea exaggerates. She knows me too well. "Looks like Sarah may have it bad for you too."

"How do you know?" I look toward Sarah's table.

"Don't look." Andrea turns her back to the dining area and steps in front of me to block my view. "Woman, you gotta play it cool."

"I am." I laugh. I peek around Andrea's head to see Marla and Ginny eyeballing me with big smiles on their faces. Sarah's back is to me. I wonder how she saw me come in. "Think Sarah is talking about me?"

"Do rabbits poop pellets?" She arches an eyebrow.

I chuckle. "Nice analogy there."

"Andrea Beckett," the hostess says. We both look her way. "Your table is ready. Follow me please." She guides us to the other side of the restaurant where I cannot see Sarah. Maybe it's for the best.

We take our seats across from each other. Andrea props her arms on the table. "Now tell me about this phone call you didn't return to Sarah." Her curiosity is piqued, and I know there is no way I'm getting out of this conversation.

I lean back in my chair, take a sip of my drink, then begin down the long road of what has been going on in my life.

CHAPTER TWELVE

"Bryn." My body moves from side to side against my own will. "Wake up!" Brayden is on my bed shaking me.

I roll onto my back. "What time is it?"

"Morning time." He gives me a cheesy smile.

"You got jokes, huh?" I grab his sides and tickle him until he squeals. I let him go to look at the time on my phone. Seven forty-five. "Could you not sleep in?"

"No. I had a bad dream." He lays down beside me.

"How about we get out of the house today? Me, you, and Ben. Maybe we get breakfast at the café and then head over to the aquarium."

"Yes!" Brayden jumps up onto his knees and clasps his hands together. "Please. Let's do that."

I smile. "Okay. Go get Ben up and you two get dressed."

Brayden leaps off the bed and runs down the hall. I'd rather him not wake Mom, though I'm sure she'll be happy to have the house to herself. She was in bed last night when I got home. Stan's car was in the driveway. I would like to avoid them both this morning, if possible.

I get up and get ready to spend the day with the boys. Tonight, I'm headed over to see Sarah. So far, I'm in a good mood. I hope to keep it that way. I can't believe Sarah invited me to her house. That seems unreal. Just the two of us there tonight. Alone. Any woman, in their right mind, with half a pulse would be nervous. Well, anyone with a crush on Sarah.

It's been really chilly lately, so I put on my favorite T-shirt with a zip-up over it, a pair of dark-wash jeans, and my favorite Converse. I pull my hair up and apply a tad bit of makeup, so I can look like I'm more rested than I am.

"Ready?" Brayden is standing in my doorway.

"Yes, sir." I grab my phone and credit card. "Look how handsome you are." He is wearing his new jeans, a flannel button-up, and his new Converse. The only problem is the cowlick on the back of his head. "Come here so I can gel your hair." He walks in and I work to get his hair styled. "All done. Grab Ben and meet me downstairs. Walk, don't run," I say to his disappearing figure.

I scribble a note to leave for Mom in case she is still sleeping. Which I pray she is. I'd text her but she rarely answers anything of mine on her phone. The boys are waiting by the door. Brayden is wide-eyed and ready to go. Ben...not so much. He looks sleepy. He was up late last night. I made him turn off his video game when I got home and sent him to bed.

I place the note on the table underneath the candle, and we quietly leave. The sun is shining bright with not a cloud in sight, so we decide to walk to our favorite retro café. The place isn't busy yet, so we snag a table by the front window. We like to people watch.

The waitress takes our order and soon returns with Ben's waffles, Brayden's pancakes, and my omelet.

"This is a fun day," Brayden says, then takes a big forkful of pancakes.

I sip my coffee feeling happy with those words. He is in a good mood today and seeming more like the Brayden I know. His lip and cheek are healing up nicely.

"You awake there, kiddo?" I squeeze Ben's shoulder.

"Yeah." He nods. "This syrupy waffle helps."

"I imagine so." I smile.

We finish our breakfast then take the bus to the aquarium. It's a good bit of time before we will get there, but the boys don't seem to mind. Ben has his earbuds in playing a video game. Brayden is talking almost nonstop to me about the penguins he can't wait to see. And the sharks. And the stingrays. I think he's a little excited.

When we arrive, we are the first ones in line. Brayden is hopping all over the place. I look over at Ben and we both smile. I know he is equally as happy as I am to have Brayden back to his chipper self.

We take our time going from exhibit to exhibit. I let the boys do whatever they want. They both feed and touch the stingrays. We take a trip on the glass-bottom boat over the sharks. Then we go through the big tunnel to see sharks and all the other fish in there with them. Before I know it, it's lunchtime. We stop and each of us get a corn dog and french fries. The boys choose a table near the shark lagoon so we can watch the fish swim.

"Look!" Brayden points to the tank. "It's a turtle." A big sea turtle swims by while we are eating.

"Pretty cool." I watch the turtle swim up and down, then out of sight again.

"I love this place. Don't you, Ben?" Brayden takes a bite of his corn dog.

"Yeah, it's awesome," Ben says. And I can tell he really is enjoying it. He may be twelve and think he's too old or cool for the things Brayden enjoys, but he likes this kind of stuff. We haven't been in a couple years, since I brought them for Ben's birthday. It's nice to have a day out with the boys.

We finish lunch and head over to see the much-anticipated penguins. Brayden drags Ben into all the tunnels to get a better look. Ben happily obliges his little brother. I sit on the bench and watch them laugh together.

My phone beeps from the inside pocket of my zip-up. I remove it and see a message from Sarah. It's her address followed by an emoji of spaghetti. I reply with a smiley face and then a

GIF of Winnie-the-Pooh sitting at a table ready to eat dinner. She sends a laughing face back and a *see you soon.*

"What are you smiling at?" Ben sits down beside me.

"Just a funny text from a friend."

"A boyfriend?" Ben wiggles his eyebrows.

"Nope. The only boys in my life are you and Brayden. And that's all I want."

"Oh, so a girlfriend." He then makes kissy faces in the air.

I playfully shove his shoulder. "Stop it."

He laughs. "I'm glad Brayden is doing better. Aren't you?"

I look over at Brayden. He is squatted down in front of a penguin. He is raising his hand up and down trying to get it to follow him. "I'm glad he's happy. He seems relaxed. How was everything last night with Mom and Stan?"

"They're getting married." Ben shakes his head, clearly in disappointment. "They took us out for pizza and told us."

"How do you feel about that?" I know how I feel, but it's more important for the boys.

"I mean he is a dork, but at least he's nice to us. Maybe he'll be a good stepdad." Ben shrugs.

"Yeah. Maybe so. He does try to include you and Brayden. I guess we should keep an open mind about him." I need to stay positive for them. Mom's mind seems to be made up. There is nothing to do but accept it and make the most out of the situation. The boys' dad will be in prison for a long time. Stealing from the company you work for will do that.

"I overheard Mom and Stan talking about turning your room into a home office for him. Are you moving out?"

Wow. It appears Mom and Stan have an agenda. She's always nagged me to stay and didn't want me to leave because of the boys. Now that she has Stan, there must not be room for me anymore. "I will someday. I haven't any plans right now."

"Good," Ben says. "I don't want you to leave." He stands up and walks over to Brayden. He gets shy with his feelings. I think it has a lot to do with Mom's persona that emotions make you weak.

I wonder when Mom plans on kicking me out. I've had this dilemma for a while now. I've wanted to leave since high school, but I stayed. I stayed for the boys because they needed me. I stay because I fear when I do leave that she will not step up like she should. I don't want any regrets when it comes to my brothers.

When we finally leave the aquarium, we go play a round of indoor putt-putt golf. After that, both boys are tired, and I need to get back so I can get ready to meet Sarah. Brayden falls asleep on the bus almost immediately. Ben dozes in and out while messing around on his phone. The bus pulls up to our stop. I pick Brayden up and carry him. Ben carries the bag of goodies I bought them at the aquarium. It only cost me an arm and a leg.

Mom and Stan are watching television when we walk in. They have all the lights out in the house, and the curtains are pulled closed. It's dark. They don't say anything when we walk in. I take Brayden upstairs and lay him down. I pull his shoes off and cover him up with a throw blanket. Ben turns on his video game. No surprise there. I take off to my room to shower so I can go meet Sarah.

* * *

"Hi," Sarah says, standing in the doorway of her two-story house. She is wearing faded denim jeans and a comfy-looking black sweater that hangs slightly off one shoulder. Her long blond hair is wavy. I haven't seen her wear it this way before. She is beautiful.

"Come in." She motions me in with a nod and a smile.

"I love your house," I say, honestly, and then push a bottle of wine forward. I picked it up on the way over. "It's a cabernet. I have no idea if it's any good."

"Thank you." Sarah smiles. "Let's find out."

I follow her to the kitchen and watch as she opens the bottle of wine. She gets two glasses from the cabinet and pours a decent amount into each.

"It smells good in here." Like warm bread and tomato sauce.

"The bread just came out of the oven. Ready to eat?" She picks up both glasses and walks toward the dining table.

Her house has an open floor plan. When I entered, it was through a tiny foyer with a bench on the left and a coatrack on the right. Straight ahead is the living room, to the right of that is the kitchen, and on the other side of the island is the dining table. The whole back wall has windows overlooking an in-ground pool.

"The boys would love that pool." I stop to look out the window at her backyard. It is fenced in with a patio directly out the door. A couch and two chairs sit next to the house with a firepit in the middle. Lounge chairs are on each side of pool.

"They are welcome to swim here during the summer. I'd love to have you all." She smiles, genuinely. "My niece and nephew are the only ones who put it to good use."

"And you. I mean, I assume because of your tan." I look away, embarrassed by my comment.

"Yes. I do love lounging by the pool in the summer. Luckily, my tan has lasted this time." She places my wineglass next to hers on the table and sits down at the end. "Come sit."

I take the seat next to her on the left and facing the windows. There is spaghetti, salad, and bread on the table.

"I'm glad you didn't eat beforehand." Sarah scoops spaghetti onto her plate. "Or you'd miss out on my famous spaghetti."

"Me too," I agree. I fix my plate with a little of everything she has out. I take my first bite of spaghetti. It's so good. Mom never cooks for us. I do all the cooking and I am not particularly good at it. We survive. "This is delicious."

"Thank you." She takes a bite of her food. I look away so not to stare at her perfect mouth. "What did you do today?"

"I took the boys to the aquarium. They loved it."

She continues to ask me questions about my day as we eat, and I answer them all. Before I know it, we are both pushing our empty plates back. I take another sip of wine.

"How do you like it?" Sarah asks, gesturing to the wine in my hand.

"It's good. Surprisingly."

She smiles softly. "See, aren't you glad you tried my wine that night?"

She is teasing me again. "I am. You've broadened my horizons."

"I did, huh?" Sarah arches one brow and it is sexy as hell.

I'm feeling all sorts of things at the moment. I stand to pick up my plate because I don't know what else to do after a moment like that. Sarah puts her hand over mine to stop my actions, and it does. I look at her nicely manicured fingers over mine and think about what it would be like for her to touch me.

"Please leave it," she says, pulling me from my thoughts. "I'll clean up later. Let's go out on the patio and have that talk."

I follow Sarah out. It's cold and a little breezy. She turns on the firepit, which is gas, and it lights up the glass rocks inside. It's very pretty. The ambience is nice right now. It feels intimate. I sit on the sofa facing the pool. Sarah sits in the wicker chair to my right. She refills both our wineglasses with the bottle she brought out. It's empty now. That went fast.

Sarah grabs a throw blanket from the back of her chair and drapes it across her lap. "Want one?"

I shake my head. "I'm fine." The fire is cozy enough to keep me warm, plus I'm used to the cold air.

"It's a nice night." She looks up at the stars. I can tell she is waiting for me to get the ball rolling, which I should do.

"It is." I take a sip of the wine, feeling the effects of it. I take a deep breath and release it. Here goes nothing. "I was eleven when Ben was born and fourteen when Brayden arrived. I've been their caretaker their whole lives. Since the age of sixteen, I've been the one taking them to doctor's appointments, helping them with homework, buying their clothes, and anything else they need. The reason I tell you this is because as their sister and the person who has been their whole world since birth, I have no say in how things get handled. I had no choice but to let Mom be in control with Brayden at school, no matter how hard I tried to change her mind. But in the end, I have failed Brayden. I don't want to do that again. That's why I need your help if that's possible. I made a promise that he wouldn't have to fight again. He believes me, and I don't want to break that promise. But I have to do this behind our mother's back."

Sarah pulls her feet up on the chair underneath her and positions her body more toward me. "You are so young to have so much responsibility. You are a good person, Brynlee. I mean that."

I feel my face heat and look down at the wine in my glass to hide it. "Thanks," I say, shyly.

"You and I can come up with a game plan tonight and I will talk to Brayden privately tomorrow. We will protect him," she says. I feel my heart squeeze at her words because I so hope she is right. "First we need a plan of action so that it doesn't get to the point of fighting. Maybe…" Sarah pauses. "Could you get him a whistle to hang around his neck in case he gets teamed up on and no one's around? That way someone can rush to help. But if they start harassing him with words, he needs to come to me immediately."

"That sounds good. It's best if you talk to him at school so Mom doesn't know I'm involved. She is all about him using his fists."

"I can do that." Sarah nods. "I was in the office when your mom came to school. The principal told her about the no fighting policy. Your mom said that she teaches her boys to use their fists."

"I'm sure she didn't like hearing that."

"No, she didn't. The principal was firm that she may have that rule at her home, but at school he has to follow those rules."

"Good. Though it won't stop her from pushing him to fight."

"Well, we can change that. But could you do something for me?"

"Anything," I say, a little too quickly. "I mean whatever you need."

"Talk to Brayden and get him to respond back to the bullies. He needs to tell them to back off, or leave him alone, and walk away like it doesn't matter. I'm hoping that if he acts like the insults don't bother him, they will eventually stop."

"You don't think he stands up for himself in those ways?"

"Unfortunately, no. He is quiet and shy."

"That doesn't sound like the kid I know. He is happy and energetic at home. You should have seen him today at the aquarium. He was hopping around, smiling, and reading about all the sea life."

"He's comfortable with you all at home. At school, he is nervous and tense. I don't think he feels like he can be himself."

I feel sad hearing this. "I just don't understand how anyone could bully Brayden."

"I don't understand it either."

I lean forward and put my head in my hands. "It's hard watching someone you love go through something like this. He's so young."

I hear Sarah get up from her seat. I don't look to see where she is going, but I see her feet disappear around the firepit. I imagine she is going inside to give me privacy. Now I feel bad for making her uncomfortable. The wine isn't helping my sad state.

"I'm so sorry," Sarah says, then I feel her hand on my back as she sits down beside me.

Goose bumps cover my body at her touch. "Thank you." I look up and out toward the pool. The crisp night air is chilly, which makes the fire feel that much better. Some of the warmth isn't from the fire, though.

"We will get through this together. Brayden will be okay." She runs her hand up my back and then down again before pulling it away.

I lean back beside her, resting my head against the sofa. "Thank you." I turn my head toward her and realize how close we are. Her eyes are so beautiful in the firelight. I've thought she was gorgeous from the moment I arrived. Actually, from the moment we met.

"You have stunning eyes," Sarah says, causing my stomach to tighten. "I'm sure you've been told that before. They're so green right now."

"Thank you." That simple compliment has made me shy all over again. I'm not sure if any other person has ever had this effect on me.

Sarah's eyes seem to light up even more. I look down at my hands. Why am I being like this? I should repay her the compliment. There are so many I could give. It's on the tip of my tongue, I just can't get the words out. My brain and my mouth are not on the same page.

Sarah reaches down, picks up her full wineglass, and takes a sip. "How's college going?"

Disappointment sets in. Sarah is an amazing person in so many ways besides being beautiful. I really wish I could tell her some of that. "It's fine. I'll be glad when it's over and I can start my career. Feels like I've been in school forever."

"Not much longer, right? It'll all be worth it in the end." Sarah's voice is confident and comforting. She has that aura about her that feels like whatever she says is the truth.

"It will." I nod. "I saw your friend Ginny not that long ago." I shift to sit up straighter. "Did she tell you?"

"She did, actually." Sarah focuses really hard on her wineglass. I thought she would say more, but she seems a little distant now that I mentioned Ginny. Did I say something wrong?

I look at my watch. I've been here a long time. I don't want to wear out my welcome. "I should get going." I stand. "I appreciate you having me over."

"I'm glad to be able to help." Sarah reaches down to shut off the firepit and stands. We are so close to each other that I can smell her perfume. Her blond hair picks up with the breeze, blowing it around her face. She takes her hand and pulls it to one side to keep it out of her face. I want to tell her how beautiful she is.

"I'll walk you out." Sarah picks up our wineglasses and turns.

I follow her inside as she takes the glasses to the sink. I quickly pull out my phone to get an Uber because I completely forgot. Ten minutes. Shit! Sarah leads me to the door where we stop just in the foyer.

"Thanks, again." I place my hand on the doorknob. "For dinner, for the talk, for being kind…"

Sarah props against the wall next to the door. "Anytime." She smiles. "I did give you my number early on. You can message me anytime, you know. I'm here if you need to talk."

"I have a weird thing about bothering people."

"No way." She shakes her head. "I wouldn't have given it to you if I thought you'd bother me. So, use it."

I smile. "Okay." I pull the door open. "Mind if I wait on your porch for my ride?"

Sarah's eyebrows shoot up instantly. "I completely forgot. Do you need a ride home?"

"No. I'm good. An Uber will be here in"—I look at my phone—"six minutes."

"I am so sorry." She steps a little closer. "I should have offered."

"This is what I do." I shrug. "I'm actually getting a car soon." I hate this feeling. For goodness' sake, most people get cars at sixteen. I am too old not to have one. I turn and walk out feeling insecure about my lack of...well, things.

"I'll wait with you." Sarah follows me and sits down on the top step. I sit beside her. She props hers her arms on her knees. "You sacrifice a lot for your brothers, don't you?"

"I..." I cross my arms over my chest. It's chilly without with the fire.

"I'm sorry. I didn't mean to..." She trails off.

"Yes. I do." I nod. "I don't regret any sacrifice I have made for them. Taking the bus or Uber isn't so bad, and it's pretty cheap since I don't travel far. Plus..." I pause a moment to look over at Sarah, who is staring at me. "I would do it all over again and more if they needed it."

"I think you are an amazing person." Sarah's cheeks are flushed pink from the night air. My heart picks up speed as we continue to make eye contact. Her blue eyes look into mine, searching for something I am unsure of but making me feel more than I have in a very long time for another person.

"I think you are pretty amazing too," I say in such a soft voice that I barely recognize it as my own.

We hear the car before we see it pull up to the curb. I look away first. Sarah stands and offers me her hand to pull me to my feet.

"Good night, Brynlee. Be safe."

"Good night," I say back.

I get in the Uber and close the door. I look back at Sarah's porch. She is still standing there watching me as we start to drive off. Her cardigan is pulled closed in the front to protect her against the night air. She smiles at me. That means more than she knows.

CHAPTER THIRTEEN

I'm standing under the pavilion in front of the school waiting for Brayden. As soon as he sees me, he takes off running.

"No running!" says a teacher who is helping direct students to the bus. He is a big, burly man with a mustache and a balding head.

Brayden puts on the brakes and comes to a stop right in front of me. "Hey!"

"Hey, little man." I put my hand on the top of his head. "Did you have a good day?"

"It was okay," he says, breathing in and out deeply from his sprint. He is exaggerating a little. I know he has more energy than that.

"Ready to go to Ben's game?"

"Yeah." He nods his head vigorously. "Can I get nachos and cheese?"

I chuckle. "Sure."

We start walking toward the middle school, which is just down the road. The high school is at the top of the hill. It makes an easy commute for families with kids in each school.

"Ms. Cain said to tell you hi." Brayden swings his arms back and forth. "I told her we were going to Ben's basketball game today."

"Oh, really?"

"Yep. I told her she could come too."

"What did she say?" I have a twinge of excitement thinking she may come. It would be nice to see her again.

"Um." Brayden looks up to the sky, as if trying to remember the conversation. "She said she couldn't make it, but she hopes Ben plays good and to tell you hello."

"You and Ms. Cain are buddies, huh?"

"She's nice. I got to help hand out papers today."

Sarah is that kind of teacher. She really cares about her students. It means a lot to me that she's helping look after Brayden.

We walk into the middle school, which enters at the main hall. Straight ahead is the gymnasium. We take the ramp to the right leading to the lunchroom, so we can get Brayden his nachos and soda. They have the curtains open along the left side of the lunchroom so people can watch the game while snacking. They don't like anyone to eat or drink in the gym since they put in a new floor.

We get Brayden's food and sit close to the opening to watch Ben. There aren't many people in the stands. Ben is warming up on the court in his white uniform with blue and red stripes down the side of this shorts. Ben is taller than most of the other boys on his team. I see him looking around for us. I wave when he looks our way. Brayden does too. Ben sees us and smiles but doesn't wave back. He has a reputation to uphold. The whistle blows and the game begins while Brayden crunches on his chips, getting cheese all over his fingers.

"There's Ms. Cain." Brayden points behind me. I turn to see Sarah walking our way. She has a red and blue backpack in her hand.

"Hi," she says, stopping at our table.

"Hi." I smile.

"Brayden, I think this belongs to you." She holds up his Spider-Man backpack.

"Oops," he says. Sarah hands him the bag, Brayden takes it and lays it beside him on the bench.

"What do you say, Brayden?"

"Thank you, Ms. Cain."

"You're welcome." Sarah smiles. "Those nachos look tasty."

"Want one?" Brayden picks up a chip and offers it to Sarah.

"Oh, no. You eat them." Sarah laughs.

"Thanks for bringing that back. I didn't realize he had left it behind."

"No problem. I was afraid he may have homework in there. Luckily, I knew where you would be." Her eyes hold mine.

"The game's just started, if you want to sit for a little while." I am hopeful she'll stay.

"Please!" Brayden chimes in. He's adorable and hard to say no to, so I'm thankful for his input. Plus, I think Sarah has a soft spot for him.

"Sure. I have a few minutes to spare." Sarah looks at Brayden. "Is this seat taken?"

He hops to his right, pulling his backpack with him. Then he dusts off the seat with his hand, cleaning it for her. It's too cute.

"Thank you," Sarah tells Brayden. Then she smiles at me, clearly amused. She is wearing her hair up in a clip. It's a little messy with wavy tendrils fallen around her face. Her speckled gray-and-brown dress slacks are still neat with only slight wrinkles. The cream-colored button-up shirt is snug and looks perfect. I imagine her body is amazing underneath those cute clothes.

"What?" Sarah smiles at me, almost like she's nervous. "Do I have something on me?" She looks down at her shirt to inspect it. I was caught staring. Geez!

"No, you're fine. My mind just wandered off." I did not just say that. I know my face is glowing right now. Perfect.

"Where'd it go?" Brayden asks and Sarah laughs at his question. My cheeks are definitely a shade of pink now. I feel them heat.

"On vacation." I wink at Brayden, hoping that's the end of my embarrassment.

"I wanna go," Brayden says. "Can Ms. Cain come too?" He looks at Sarah.

Sarah's eyes glisten with amusement as she turns to look at me. "Where is this vacation?"

"In a land far, far away," I say.

"Like Shrek!" Brayden says, excitedly.

Sarah laughs again. "You're a funny guy."

"He is," I agree.

Brayden smiles really big, showing his teeth and squinting all silly like.

"Ben just scored." I point toward the court. Anything to take the attention off me. Plus, I realize we haven't been paying attention to the game.

"What's his number?" Sarah searches for him.

"Twenty-three." Brayden points to Ben underneath the goal.

Ben gets the rebound and he is back down the court again. I watch Sarah watching Ben. The more I'm around her, the more I admire her. Her ex must be crazy to not do everything in her power to keep her. I look away right as Sarah catches me looking at her. I feel her eyes on me, but I keep watching the game.

"I have to get going," Sarah says. "I have dinner plans tonight." I wonder who those plans are with. I guess I assumed she was single, but maybe she is dating someone. That's an image I don't want to think about.

"Bye, Ms. Cain," Brayden says loudly.

"Take good care of that backpack. Spider-Man is important." Sarah pats his shoulder.

"I will." He pulls his backpack a little closer to his side.

"Thanks again," I say, a little sullen that she is leaving, and also hoping it's a family dinner. Not that it matters if I never get the nerve to make a move or let her know that I'm attracted to her.

"It was no problem." Sarah stands and steps a little behind Brayden. Her eyes grow wide as she motions to Brayden with her head and mouths the words, *talk to him.*

I nod. "Have a nice dinner."

She flashes me a wink before she passes by, and lightly touches my shoulder. "Bye," she says. If she only knew what she was doing to me.

I wait a minute before turning to see that she has gone. Brayden and I watch the rest of the half from the lunchroom, then we head to the bleachers. I skipped out on class tonight to be here for Ben. Brayden leads us up the bleachers to the very top against the wall. Our seat is far enough away from the other people that no one can hear us if we talk. I'm happy for that.

"Hey, little man," I say, then exhale a calming breath. "I want to talk to you about something." He looks up at me but doesn't say anything. "When the boys at school bully you, do you tell them to stop?" He looks down at his hands and instantly his demeanor changes. "I'm not going to be upset with you. I need to know so I can help."

"I'm scared," he says, nervously.

"Scared of the boys at school, or scared to talk to me?" For all I know he could be talking about our mother, and afraid to upset her.

"The boys." He kicks his feet against the bleachers, shaking them a little. I put my hand on his leg to stop him.

"Look what I got for you today." I pull out a whistle that is attached to a necklace. I slide it over his head, so it dangles down his chest. "If those bullies try to fight you again, you blow this whistle so a teacher can come help you."

He picks up the whistle and examines it. "Can I blow it now?"

"Not yet." I laugh. "But when we leave school, most definitely."

He turns the whistle around in his hand to examine it, then I see a hint of a smile.

"I was also thinking that maybe you could do something else for me." Brayden stops looking at the whistle and raises his head to me. "When those boys say mean things to you, tell them to stop or back off. Then you turn and walk away like their words mean nothing to you. I know deep down inside here"—I tap his chest—"you might be scared. But you will have the whistle to alert someone if they try anything. Can you be brave for me?"

Brayden's lip quivers. "I don't want to fight anymore. It hurt."

"No way, Jose. You do not have to fight." I shake my head. "I only want you to use your words."

He nods. "Ms. Cain talked to me today."

"She did?" I am so relieved to hear this. Sarah is the best. But I already knew this about her. She is becoming someone I can count on.

"Yep. She said that she wants me to tell her anything Adam and Jackson say that's bad. And that if they bump me to go tell her."

"Good. That's what you should do. Tell them to back off, or leave you alone, then go tell Ms. Cain. If they push you or try to fight, then you have the whistle." I pick it up for emphasis. "I'm proud of you."

He nods.

"I love you," I say, then pull him into a side hug.

"I love you too." He leans his body into me while holding the whistle tight in his hand.

Ben comes out of the locker room and we spend the second half cheering him on. I feel more at ease having talked to Brayden about everything. Sarah really came through for us.

* * *

"Long time, no see, stranger." Damon twists in his seat to face me as I enter class. He is all smiles as I slide into the seat across from him.

"I only missed one class." I roll my eyes. "Thank you for the notes, by the way." I did message the teacher to let him know I'd be out.

"No problem. It was super slow. A few other people were out. Not much happened."

I take out my notebook and place it beside my computer. "It's been a long week and it's only Tuesday."

"Tell me about it. I've had a lot of extra shifts at work. I'm going to make bank on my next paycheck."

"Awesome! Drinks on you, then."

Damon smiles. "I can manage that. Speaking of, when are you going to come out and listen to my friend's band? You never responded back."

"Oh, shoot. I'm so sorry. I completely forgot. I've had a lot going on at home. But I most definitely want to check out the band. When are they playing next?"

"Um…" Damon pulls out his phone and scrolls through it. "I'm not sure. I'll message Sydney and let you know."

"Sounds good. Are you and this Sydney more than friends?" I wiggle my eyebrows.

He chuckles. "No. She's dating someone. Plus, I've known her for, like forever. I don't see her that way."

"Gotcha. Well, let me know."

"Will do." Damon turns on his computer. "So, how did your page turn out? Mine is spot-on."

We compare our work while we wait on the teacher to come in. My mind drifts to Sarah. She occupies a lot of my thoughts lately.

* * *

"Ready for the bus?" The boys have just finished their cereal and are slow-poking around. "Leave your bowls and go brush your teeth."

They take off racing each other upstairs. I put the bowls in the dishwasher and wipe up the spilled milk. I have already done my morning routine, so I'm ready to go.

While the boys are finishing up, I walk to Mom's room and peek through the open door. Her bed is still made. She didn't come home last night. I didn't get the courtesy of a call or text to let me know. I assume she stayed over at Stan's.

"Boys?" I call from the bottom of the stairs. "We have to go."

I hear their footsteps as they run from the bathroom down the hall. Then they both come hurtling down the stairs, Ben leading the way.

"Beat ya," Ben says to Brayden, who sticks out his tongue.

I walk them out to catch the bus, as I do almost every morning. As we wait, I hear the distinct sounds of Stan's noisy truck from behind us, as well as an unfamiliar clattering. I turn to see it coming down the road. They pull into the driveway of the house. There are cans tied to the back of his truck with a *Just Married* sign in the back window. Ben and Brayden look up at me just as surprised as I am.

"Guess Mom got married last night," I utter. I now know why she didn't come home.

The bus pulls up to get the boys. I hang around long enough to wave bye to Brayden, then I take off on my walk to the bus stop. I don't turn around even when I hear the truck door slam and Mom laughing. If I were a betting woman, I'd put money on them still being drunk from last night. I assume they took the day off from work, considering. It's unlike Mom to miss work. But, of course, we are talking about a man she did this for. That's a whole different story.

I zip up my jacket and warm my hands in the pockets of my jeans as I walk. I must have been walking slower than normal because I arrive at the same time as the bus. I take the seat behind the driver. It seems to be the warmest, and I'm very cold at the moment. Whether it's from the weather or my mom's news, I'm not sure. I think about texting Sarah. I've thought about it every day since I last saw her. The thing is, I don't know what to say.

Andrea is waiting for me when I exit the bus. "You look spiffy." I whistle. "Big plans after work?"

"I'm only working a half day today. Got to go get Momma at lunch and take her to the doctor. Daddy is down in his back and can't get around."

We walk into work behind other people showing up for their shift. "You must be in the office again today. I miss you on the line."

"I miss you too, boo. But I'm livin' large with my own desk and coffeepot." Andrea does a little dance to show her excitement. "Plus, you'll be leaving me soon for a big fancy job. I need to move up to management."

I stop walking abruptly and grab her arm. "There was a posting yesterday for management. I overheard them talking about Bill leaving."

"Shut up!" Andrea's eyes go wide. "I'm all over it like flies on cow shit."

"You have a way with words." I laugh.

"Thank you." Andrea gives a small curtsey.

I shake my head and walk away from her in dramatic fashion.

"Hey." Andrea chases after me. "Don't leave me behind."

"Well, come on, then." I look over my shoulder at her and stick out my tongue.

"Save that thing for Ms. Sexy Teacher Lady." Andrea laughs as she catches up to me.

"Her name is Sarah." I punch in on the time clock.

"Oh, Ms. Sa-rah, then," Andrea says in an old proper Southern voice. I laugh. She then holds her timecard between her first two fingers, lifting her other fingers out like she is drinking fancy tea. and punches in.

"Enjoy your half day in that cozy little office. And tell your parents I said hi."

"I can do both those things." She waves. "Text you later."

Andrea and I go our separate ways. I drop my stuff at my locker, then head to get the day started. A mindless session of work. I can get behind that.

CHAPTER FOURTEEN

The boys are riding the bus today, so I'm able to go straight home from work. It's about another hour before they will get out of school. I get off the bus a couple blocks away and make my way toward home. Stan's truck is gone from the driveway. Mom's car is here. Maybe he went into work after all.

I go in through the kitchen and quickly realize that no one is home. All the lights are off and it's quiet. Mom would be watching television or sitting at the dining table if she were here. I flip on the light as I make my way to the fridge. I am so thirsty. There is only one soda and one Gatorade remaining. I need to go to the store. I close the fridge and get a glass of water instead. The boys usually raid the fridge when they get home from school.

Screech! The sound of tires in the driveway is loud. Then I hear three doors slam followed by Mom's raised voice. What in the world is going on?

The back door opens. "Get inside," Mom snarls. Ben and Brayden move past her with their heads hung low. I hear Stan's truck backing out of the driveway. "This day is ruined. It was supposed to be a happy day with me relaxing with my husband. But no, I had to get up and go to the school once again!" Mom raises her eyes to see me standing at the refrigerator. "And what the fuck is this?" She rears back and throws something at my head. I duck. It bounces off the wall and breaks in front of me. It's Brayden's whistle.

"What the hell?" I lift my head back up.

Brayden starts crying.

"Go to your room." Mom points at the boys. Ben takes Brayden by the arm to lead him away. He passes me a worried glance as they hurry by.

I want to go after the boys, to comfort them, but feel I need to stay here for the moment. Mom is on fire, and I'd rather her aim be at me. "What's going on?"

"I'll tell you what's going on. You gave Brayden a damn whistle so he can be a little wimpy-ass kid and call for help. So, therefore, some goody-two-shoes woman comes to his rescue and I had to go back to the school to hear her tell me how I should handle my own kid. Like she is his damn parent or something." Mom stomps over to the fridge, nudges me out of the way, and gets the only soda in there. "Did I not tell you to stay out of it?" She pushes her finger into my chest. I don't move. That would only encourage her. She turns, not seeming to want to waste her time on me, and grabs a bottle of whiskey from the counter. She pours two fingers' worth and then half the soda over it. Her ranting continues. She talks about the principal, downgrading him. Then she starts in on Sarah, doing the exact same thing. By the time she is done ranting, I've learned very little. But what I do know is that the two boys who have been bullying Brayden were suspended today for threatening him and pushing him down. Brayden finally spoke up for himself in the principal's office. The boys are under a strict warning that all bullying is to stop or there will be further consequences. While I'm happy with the results, Mom seems to feel as though she has been attacked for her method of parenting.

"I won't tell you again to stay out of this with Brayden," she says. She picks up her drink and downs the contents. "No more chances." She glares at me while pouring her second fix.

"Okay." I agree, though her threats are meaningless. I will always help Brayden or Ben if they need it. I turn and walk away, leaving Mom to her alcohol. I have class tonight, but I'm not going. Mom has never been violent with the boys and I don't think she would be, but I still don't feel comfortable leaving them alone while she is on a rampage and in the whiskey.

When I reach the boys' room, the door is shut. It's not often they close it. I lightly tap on it to make sure they aren't changing. The door swings open. Ben is standing behind it.

"Come in," he says, then closes the door behind me.

Brayden is lying on his bed facedown. I sit beside him. "Are you okay? Did you get hurt?"

Ben slides down against the bedroom door and sits on the floor. He puts his head in his hands. "He's not talking."

"Brayden?" I rub my hand up and down his back. Still no answer. "I'm so proud of you," I say, trying to get him to open up. "You did exactly what I asked, and now those boys are in trouble."

He turns his face to the side so I can see his eyes. They are wet with tears.

"I know that right now you are scared and out of sorts, but you are going to be okay. Things will get better. Didn't Ms. Cain come help you immediately when you blew the whistle?" He nods his head, then reaches up and wipes his nose. I see Ben out of the corner of my eye raise his head to watch us. "So, tell me why you're upset right now. I want to help."

He rolls over onto his back and wipes his eyes on the sleeve of his shirt. "'Cause Mom tried to hurt you."

My heart squeezes. "But I'm okay. I was good at dodgeball in school." I smile and turn my head to the side, trying to make him smile. It doesn't work. "Come give me a hug." He practically lunges into my arms. "You too." I wave for Ben to join us.

"I'm good." Ben shakes his head.

"Benjamin Jay Foster, get up here now. This is a family hug."

Ben reluctantly gets up and wraps his arms around us both for a few seconds before pulling away. He sits next to us on the bed.

"Are you hurt anywhere?" I pull Brayden's arms from around my neck so I can look him in the face.

"Right here." He points to his side. "They kicked me after I blew the whistle, and then they ran."

"Let me look." I lift his shirt. Brayden points to the red area on his side. "Is it sore?" I gently run my hand over it. He nods. I notice Ben watching us. He's acting strange. Almost distant. I reach out and touch his forearm. "Are you okay?"

Ben shrugs. He turns his head away. He stares out the window ahead. I'm sure this is a lot for him to process too. He has a tender heart no matter how hard he tries not to show it.

"I'm not going to school tonight. I'm going to go get some food from the store. When I get back, we can eat dinner and play some Wii. I'll get some snacks. Gummy bears, Reese's cups, and…"

"Skittles?" Brayden says.

I smile. "Of course. Ben what about you? Any preference?"

He shrugs his shoulders again.

"Ben, do you want some Starburst?" Brayden asks. "That's his favorite, Bryn."

"Okay. Starburst it is. If you can think of anything else, just text me. I won't be too long."

When I get downstairs, Mom is still sitting at the table with what looks like a fresh drink. She must be on the verge of drunk now, having consumed so much so quick.

"Can I borrow the car? I'm going to get groceries." There is barely anything in the house to eat or drink. I was holding out hope Mom would go, but I lost that battle.

Mom tosses me the keys. "Don't you have college tonight?"

"They canceled class," I lie. I'd rather not hear her get snarky with me about staying home. She'll know it's for the boys, and then I'd get an earful.

"Grab Stan some Natural Light." She slurs a little, confirming what I already knew.

I nod as I pass by. She doesn't offer to give me any money. She never does. A couple hours later and I'm pulling back into the driveway with a carload of groceries. I send Ben a text and ask him to meet me outside to help carry everything in. Stan still isn't here.

I pop the trunk and grab a few bags. The back door opens and both boys come outside to help. "Where's Mom?" I ask.

"In her room," Ben says.

"Here." I hand him the bag of snacks. "Take this to your room quickly so Mom doesn't see." If we don't hide the candy, she'll throw out remarks about me spoiling them, or how I shouldn't reward Brayden for his behavior. I'm sure I could think of more, but I just don't care to try.

Ben hurries upstairs while Brayden and I get the last few bags of groceries. "Thank you, Brayden." I smile. He places the bags on the floor and begins getting the items out, putting them on the table. Ben comes back and helps him.

I make dinner for everyone and we all eat. Mom doesn't join us. She's probably sleeping off her whiskey high, and I prefer that. We finish up and I send the boys upstairs so I can clean up and join them afterward. I pull out my phone and type up a message to Sarah. I hover over the send button. I can't bring myself to do it. Then my phone beeps. It's Damon. *Where are you?*

Sorry, family stuff tonight. Couldn't make it, I reply back.

No probs. Want me to send you the notes? Damon offers, and I'm grateful for it. I didn't want to ask him to help me out again.

Please and thank you, I text back.

I erase the message I had started to Sarah and retype a simple, *Thank you.* I want her to know I appreciate what she did for Brayden today.

She replies almost instantly. *You're welcome. You've been on my mind. Hope all is okay.*

Those words resonate with me. I feel such a connection with Sarah. I want to call her and tell her everything and have her tell me it will be okay. When she says it, I believe her. But the boys need my full attention tonight. I'm determined to give them that. I send off one quick message to Sarah and simply reply with, *It is*. Then I head upstairs to the boys.

* * *

"Let's have a coloring contest," Aimee says. She is standing in front of me with a coloring book and crayons.

"I'd love to. Who's the judge?"

"Me!" Aimee says and then smiles, showing off all her teeth.

"All right," I say. "But I have to warn you, I'm pretty darn good at it." Aimee giggles.

"Stop lying to my child." Andrea walks in the room putting earrings in her ears. "You know you color outside the lines."

I laugh. "And how do you know that?"

Andrea arches her brow and places her hand on her hip. I can read her mind with that single expression.

"Aimee, do not listen to your mother."

"How are you gonna tell my child not to listen to me? Next time she misbehaves, you're coming over here and dealing with it."

"Deal." I smile. "Aimee would never misbehave. Isn't that right?" I tickle her side and she wiggles away with a squeal.

"Thanks for helping me out," Andrea's tone is serous now. "I'll be back in a couple hours."

"Anytime. I've got you." I use the same words she has said to me on many occasions. And I mean them right back.

We wave to Andrea as she leaves to go pick up her dad. His back is still giving him trouble, so she is taking him to urgent care for an x-ray and hopefully some meds to help with the muscle spasms. Andrea's usual sitter is out of town this weekend, so she messaged me this morning and asked if I could help her out. I left the boys asleep as I snuck out.

Aimee and I color away while cartoons play on the television in the background. Five Disney princess pages later and I hear a text message come through. It's Damon telling me his friend's band is playing tonight and invites me to go. I almost decline, but then I have a thought.

Mind if I bring a friend? I respond.

Bring away, he replies. *Need a ride tonight?*

I shoot back with, *I'm good.*

"Look." Aimee holds up the picture she colored. "I made my frog blue." She giggles.

"Blue frogs are the best," I say. "Nice job." Aimee smiles at me and goes back to coloring.

I pull up Sarah's name in my messages before I can overthink it. *Plans tonight? If not, want to go listen to a band? I promised Damon I'd go hear his friend play.*

"Are you hungry?" I ask Aimee. It's close to lunch and I'm sure she has been up since seven. Andrea tells me how she hasn't been able to sleep past that time since she was pregnant.

"Yes." She nods.

"Let's go to the kitchen and find something."

"Can I have a peanut butter and jelly sandwich?" Aimee hops up and skips ahead of me.

"Absolutely!" I gather the ingredients and start making the sandwich. I hear my phone alert me to a new text message from the living room. I feel a nervousness creep in. I cut the sandwich in half and place it on the table in front of Aimee. "Want some chips or anything else?"

"A juice box, please." Aimee takes a bite of her sandwich and sways from side to side.

I grab the drink from the fridge. "Here you go, baby girl. I'll be right back." I make a beeline for my phone. I wish I could be patient and play it cool, but the message is all I can think about.

That sounds like fun, Sarah's text says. I smile broadly. I almost want to do a happy dance, but I refrain from that. Aimee would think I bumped my head or something.

Great! I'll text you later when I have all the details, I reply back.

I'll call Damon in a few and find out the when, where, and what time. I head back to the kitchen. "How's that sandwich treating you?" Aimee smiles before taking another big bite.

CHAPTER FIFTEEN

"This is a cool place," I say to Damon. He is standing next to me at the bar. We are ordering drinks.

"I know, right? Hopefully, you can meet Sydney at intermission."

I arrived about ten minutes ago. Damon was waiting out front for me. The band has been on stage tuning their equipment since then. Seems like they will start any minute now. I glance toward the door for the umpteenth time. Damon follows my eyes.

"Is your friend late?" he asks.

I look at my watch. "No. We agreed on eight o'clock. She has a few minutes."

Behind us, the lead singer starts talking. "Hope everyone is ready for a good time tonight." He strums his guitar. "I always love starting the night off with this cover. Hope you enjoy it as much as I do."

"They are good." I raise my voice so Damon hears me over the music. Right as the band front man sings, "She's beautiful," Sarah walks through the door. And it couldn't be more perfect.

Took the words straight from my mind. She is looking around for me. And for a moment I just watch her, taking in her beauty. Her eyes roam the room until they finally make it to my direction. I lift my arm to get her attention. Her smile is wide and glorious.

Sarah walks up and stands in front of me and Damon. "Hi, again," she says to Damon.

"Hello." He smiles. "Glad you could make it." He glances over at me with a mischievous look. I never told him who I invited. He didn't ask. But I do know he thinks she's pretty.

"We are just about to order a drink," I say. "That is, if we can get her attention. What would you like?"

"I'll take a Cosmo," Sarah says. Her eyes are stunningly blue. Someone could get lost in them. I can feel the guard I hold up slipping away the more I'm around her. Whatever happens will happen. Sarah said yes to coming out with me tonight. Not to talk about Brayden. But to hang out with me and listen to some music. I feel like that has to mean something.

Damon flashes some cash toward the bartender and catches her eye. He turns his head toward us and speaks out the side of his mouth. "The trick is to tip really well the first time, so they remember you."

"What can I get you?" The bartender says to Damon.

"A Yuengling, Cosmo, and…" He looks to me.

"An old-fashioned," I supply. I enjoyed it when I had it for the first time with Andrea, and it was different. I want to try it again.

The bartender points at me. "I need to see your ID."

Damon snickers as he passes my license to her and then back to me. "Here you go, youngin'." He laughs.

Sarah leans close, a smile spreading across her face. "Barely legal."

"You two having fun giving me hell?"

"Of course." Damon shakes his head. "Though I didn't peg you for a whiskey drinker."

I am my mother's daughter. The thought rushes to my head.

"No Jack and Coke tonight, then." Sarah's eyes flicker with amusement. She remembered what I drink.

"I may even be adventurous later tonight and try something besides whiskey." I tilt my head to the side, lifting my shoulders in that who-knows type of way.

Damon chuckles. "Well, I'm glad I'm here to witness this special occasion. I say let's have one hell of a night." Our drinks arrive and Damon hands them to us. He raises his beer bottle. "To new friends." We all tap our drinks together. "Let's drink!" he says.

I keep my eyes on Sarah as she takes her first sip. I can't believe she is here with me.

"You have to try this." Sarah pushes her drink toward me. "You're branching out tonight, remember?"

I laugh. "That's right. But you have to try me. Mine! I mean." I feel my cheeks and neck flush with that flub.

Sarah's eyes go wide and her smile matches. "If you say so." My stomach tightens with the thought of her meaning more than my drink.

I'm vaguely aware of Damon's eyes on us. I shift my gaze to his as I take a sip of Sarah's brightly colored drink. "I like this. Sweet, though."

"This is not." Sarah squinches up her face and hands me the drink back. "I am not a whiskey drinker."

"Want to try?" I offer Damon my drink, not wanting to leave him out.

"Sure." He takes a big drink. "Not bad. I could give it a go."

"So, Damon's friend is the drummer." I point to the stage, and Sarah turns her head to glance at the band. "Her name is Sydney. We haven't met yet."

"I love this type of music. Thanks for the invite." She looks from me to Damon. Sarah is wearing light-wash jeans with black booties. She has on a black button-up shirt with the buttons big for style with two pockets on each side of her chest. She has her sleeves rolled up a little past her wrist. Her blond hair is straight, and she has the left side pushed behind her ear.

"Where are my manners?" Damon stands. "Take my seat. I'll stand."

"Oh, no. I'm fine." Sarah waves him away.

"While that is true, you should still take a seat." Damon grins. He's flirting. I feel a small pang of jealousy creep in but push it away.

"Thank you." Sarah moves toward the stool next to me, placing her hand on my thigh as she climbs onto her seat. My body reacts to that simple touch. I look down at her perfectly manicured nails as she pulls her hand away.

"How is school going, Damon? Are you keeping Brynlee in line?" Sarah flashes me a smile.

"If she'll stop missing class, I could." Damon points at me with a click of his tongue.

"It's only been twice." I shift in my seat, uncomfortable with him calling me out. "But Damon has helped me with the notes, so I'm good now."

"Good thing she has me," he teases. "She may be top in the class now, but I'm hot on her trail. She better watch it, I might take that spot soon."

"You wish." I take a drink of my old-fashioned and stare him down over the top.

Damon chuckles. "I'll be right back." He slides his beer onto the counter between us and takes off toward the restrooms.

I focus on the band. Now that Sarah and I are alone, I'm feeling a little nervous. The bar is full of people, yet I am hyper aware of Sarah's presence. I tap my foot to the beat of the music as the band plays a different song. It feels as though Sarah's eyes are on me. I don't look toward her, but it isn't long before I feel her lean in. She presses her breast against my arm as her cheek rests just inches away from mine. My heart thumps hard against my chest.

"Is everything okay at home?" she says, her breath tickling my ear. "You all have been on my mind."

Just another reason why I am so attracted to Sarah. Not only is she physically beautiful, but she has a kind heart. I turn to face her. We are so close that the butterflies in my stomach flutter. I have a moment of being brave pushing through. The band is loud, so I let my cheek touch hers as I lean over to speak into her ear the same way she did me. "It's been tough, but I'm happy you helped Brayden. I owe you more than you know." I pull back just far enough to look into her bright blue eyes. They remind me of the bluest sky on the clearest day. Her eyes drop to my lips. My heart almost stops. Sarah does have feelings for me, whatever they may be. It's clear to me now.

"I'm back," Damon says, causing us to jerk back from each other. He reaches between us and takes his beer. "Did I miss anything?"

Boy, did he ever. "Just that I'm about to get another drink," I say. I toss back the rest of my cocktail quickly. "Anyone else?" I croak out.

Damon laughs. "Hell, yeah!" He chugs the rest of his beer. "Sarah, want another?"

"I'm still working on this one." She holds up her almost full glass.

"Here." Damon pulls out his wallet to give me some cash.

I place my hand over his. "No way. This round is on me."

"Hot damn!" He puts his wallet back in his pocket. "This night just keeps getting better. An adventurous Brynlee, free drinks, and two beautiful women. I'm a lucky guy." I don't quite care for his comment too much. It somehow rubs me the wrong way, but I can't say how.

I move closer to Sarah, but nowhere near as close as before, so she can hear me. "Better hurry up with that drink. I'm ordering you another."

"Are you trying to get me drunk?" Sarah narrows her eyes in a teasing way.

I swallow. "Not at all. But Damon said we are drinking tonight. You got to keep up." I turn to try and catch the bartender's gaze. Why couldn't I have had a funny or flirty comeback? I was shocked by her comment and then nothing. I shake my head lightly in disappointment of my actions.

"Let me help." Damon steps between Sarah and I to get to the bar. It's a tight squeeze. "You got to hold it out like this," he says.

I lightly punch his shoulder. "You've got to give me a chance next time. Are you that anxious for a new drink?"

He shakes his empty beer bottle. "Yes." I look over at Sarah, who is leaning away from Damon and focused on the band.

Damon gets the bartender's attention, and she gets to him quick. He hands me a Tito's and cranberry this time. I squeeze my lime over the ice and stir. Not sure mixing liquor is the best decision, but I'll go slow this round. I'm not about a hangover tomorrow.

We spend the next couple hours chatting away about everything and nothing. Damon mostly carries the conversation. We even sing loudly a few times with the band. Well, mainly Damon and me. He keeps finding ways to lean closer to us or say something in my ear. I blame it on the alcohol. He has consumed more than both Sarah and I combined. I've slowed down quite a bit, though I do have a nice buzz going. I have also finished a couple glasses of water. Damon hasn't touched any. Sarah is drinking very slowly. I understand, since she has to drive home.

"Hell, yes!" Damon startles me. He then starts moving his body in front of us, in what I assume is his version of dancing. Hard to be sure with his lack of rhythm. "This is my jam. Come on." He reaches his hand out to me. "Let's dance."

"Is that what you call that?" I gesture up and down his body. Sarah laughs.

"Yes." His hand is still dangling in front of me. "Come on."

"Nah. I'm fine here."

"You said you'd be adventurous tonight. Don't back out now." He reaches for my hand again.

"I said that about drinks." He doesn't listen, and instead takes my hand and tugs it forward. "Peer pressure is not fun." I hop down and turn to Sarah. "Please come with us."

She shakes her head. "You go. I'll hold our seats."

Damon still has a hold of my hand and leads me to the dance floor. Thank goodness there are other people out here. I have rhythm but I don't like to be watched.

We start dancing in front of each other, not touching at first. Then Damon takes my hand as we dance, holding it up to the side. Next thing I know he is turning me around, trying to dance up on me like we are a couple. Hell, no. I turn back around and push my hands on his chest. I shake my head and laugh to play it off. I glance toward Sarah at the bar, who is watching us. When she sees me looking, she averts her eyes and lifts her drink to her mouth. The song ends quickly, which I couldn't be happier about, and another starts.

"'Tennessee Whiskey!' I love this song!" Damon stops my progress of leaving by grabbing my arm and whipping me around a little too rough. I stumble forward so hard that he catches me. "One more," he says. He is being weird and pushy. I don't like it. Maybe he doesn't do well with liquor. I've noticed a change since he started on it.

"I'd rather go back," I say as he steps into my space and puts his hands on my waist. He starts swaying to the music.

"After this. I promise. Please, our last one."

I'm uncomfortable now. I look over at Sarah. She is watching us full-on and doesn't look away. Her brows look furrowed, but I'm buzzed and it's hard for me to be sure. I motion for her to join us. I don't think she will, but then she stands up and starts walking our way.

Sarah steps up beside me, lifting Damon's arm off my waist and pushing him off me. "This is a great song," she says as we make a triangle to dance. She puts one of her arms on my lower back, and the other on Damon's. We follow her lead.

"Now I'm definitely going to be the envy of all the guys." He belts out the words to the song. His head is held high. I pass Sarah a look of gratitude. She moves her fingers to grab my hand on Damon's back and holds it. Her eyes never leave mine. She gives me the slightest smile. My hand stays wrapped in hers behind Damon's back for the entire song. Even though Damon is here, I feel happy to have her touch me.

"That was fun," Damon says after the song ends. "Time for another drink." He whirls around to head back to the bar, leaving us to follow.

Sarah and I walk slowly behind, neither of us saying anything. One of our seats has been taken. Damon is in the other one, talking to the bartender again. He's been tipping well, so she has been very attentive to him.

"I'll be right back." Sarah touches my arm. She walks off toward the restrooms.

"Here ya go, milady." Damon stands, giving me his seat. He places a fresh drink in front of me.

"Hey, you got to stop this. I'm going to be drunk soon." I'm not one hundred percent sure that I'm not now.

"And what would that hurt?" He leans against my legs. This touchy-feely style of his tonight is not something I'm enjoying. We're friends. I don't want that ruined by the weirdness I'm feeling.

"My head, tomorrow."

He laughs. "Well, wake up to someone handsome and that could make all the difference."

"You are full of yourself." I shake my head, then turn to see if Sarah is on her way back yet.

"You like it," he says. And now I know without a doubt he is wasted. "Come here. I've got to tell you something." I don't move, not wanting to him to tell me anything. But he leans forward and puts his mouth next to my ear. I wait for him to speak, hoping he hurries. Instead of words, he kisses my cheek.

"Damon!" I turn toward him. He then presses his lips to mine forcefully. I push him away. "Don't." He stumbles back a little, and that's when I see Sarah. She is standing across the room watching us. My heart drops to my stomach. Her face says it all, and it isn't good.

Sarah turns and heads toward the exit. I push past Damon to go after her. Damon calls out my name as I call out for Sarah. I can't believe he did this to me tonight. Did I lead him on? I don't think I did. I've never given him any sign that I liked him in any way other than a friend.

I push through the front doors and see Sarah up ahead. "Sarah!" I call out. I am right behind her on the sidewalk. She is walking fast. "Where are you going?"

"I have an early start tomorrow," she calls back, barely turning her head toward me. "I'm sorry. I shouldn't have come tonight. I just thought…" She shakes her head but doesn't finish that sentence.

"Sarah, please wait. Damon kissed me. I didn't want him to." I try to explain, but she keeps walking at a steady pace.

"I misunderstood some things. It's fine."

I reach out and take Sarah's hand, pulling her to a stop. "I don't like Damon," I say as she turns to look at me.

Sarah looks down at the ground. "It's none of my business." It's the first time she has ever looked vulnerable to me. She tries to walk off again, but I tug the hand I'm still holding. She turns to face me, this time she's looking me straight in the eyes. I know it's now or never.

"I want you," I whisper. My heart is pounding in my chest. We are staring at each other. Sarah seems to be searching for the truth. Then, as I feel like she may try to leave again, she takes my hand and pulls me to the side of a building, near the alley. Her mouth finds mine instantly. I moan into the kiss as I pull her closer, my hands around her waist. Sarah's soft lips deepen the kiss, her tongue brushing against mine. I feel weak all over. My body is vibrating.

Sarah pulls back, her eyes the darkest I've ever seen them. "Come home with me," she says. I feel the intensity behind her words all the way down to the pit of my stomach.

"Yes," I reply, without hesitation. I know what I want. I'm not going to let it pass me by.

Sarah takes my hand, leading me to her car. She unlocks the doors, and we climb inside. I feel my body on high alert in anticipation of what is to come. She puts the car in drive and we are on our way. I slide my hand into hers, intertwining our fingers. She looks at me, desire clear on her face. I push up on the middle console, kissing her quickly, sucking on her bottom lip before pulling away. She sighs. It's a good sigh. I know exactly how she feels.

CHAPTER SIXTEEN

I'm not sure how we make it into Sarah's house. That all seems a blur to me. But Sarah has pushed me up against the door in the foyer. Her hands are under my shirt and her mouth on mine. She tastes sweet, like the drink she had earlier. I'm breathing hard. We both are.

I reverse our positions, putting Sarah's back against the wall. I run my lips lightly over her mouth, and she tries to come after me for more but I don't let her. I kiss down her neck, unbuttoning the first button on her shirt. I kiss the spot it touched. I unbutton the next one and kiss again. The top part of Sarah's bra is showing. I lower my mouth to her cleavage. Her hands go into my hair, her breath hitches as I pull down her bra and take a nipple in my mouth. I make quick work of the rest of the buttons, exposing her tan stomach and black bra. I run my hand down her neck, between her breasts, and over her stomach. "You are so beautiful."

She takes my hand and leads me down the hall. Her bedroom is huge. All of her furniture is white. It shows up well even with only the light from the moon shining through the window. Sarah stops at the side of the bed and turns to me. She drops her shirt and bra to the floor, releasing her full breasts. Her fingers find the hem of my shirt and pull it over my head. I reach back and release my bra, letting it fall off my arms. Sarah's eyes are all over me. My heart races as I watch her take me in. She steps backward to sit on the edge of the bed. I walk to her, standing between her legs. She reaches out and grabs my waist, pulling me closer. Her hands run up my stomach and over my breasts. Sarah's eyes hold mine as she takes my nipple in her mouth, moving from one to the other. My breathing hitches with the sensation. Her hands on my hips hold me steady as her mouth continues to work my breasts. I'm so turned on. I just want to push her back on the bed and have my way with her, but I'm letting Sarah take the lead. She unbuttons my pants and pushes them and my underwear down around my ankles. I step out of them and crawl on the bed with Sarah, following her as she crawls backward toward the pillows.

I pull her bottoms off in one swift movement and toss them to the floor. I lower myself between her spread legs. The moment our naked bodies touch, Sarah lets out a moan. I'm in awe of her body, of her sounds. It's everything and more than I expected it to be.

Sarah pulls my mouth to hers urgently, our tongues intertwining perfectly as if we have kissed a thousand times before. I push my body into her center, grinding against her. She moans into my mouth, urging me on. I shift one of my legs to straddle hers and reach between us to touch her center. She is so wet, and it turns me on so much that I can barely take it. I slide my fingers inside, moving in and out, keeping my body in rhythm with the thrusts. Sarah grabs my ass, pulling me deeper inside her with my motions. I gasp at how incredible she feels. She is breathing heavy, her breath hitching as she tightens around me. She holds me close, our foreheads connected. I pull my head back to look in her eyes. It's the most turned on I've ever been.

Sarah kisses me deeply, then she rolls us over so that she is on top. She kisses down my chest, over my stomach. Her fingers find me at the same time as her mouth. I'm almost undone. I moan as she touches me with expert hands. I reach down and lace my fingers into her hair. I roll my head to the side, my eyes closing as I reach my high.

Sarah kisses the inside of my thigh, and then my stomach as she makes her way back up to me. She brings the sheet with her to cover our bodies. I turn onto my side so that we are facing each other. She is breathing heavy.

"You," Sarah says, then kisses my shoulder. "Are so sexy." She sighs, and then pushes my hair behind my ear.

My heart is pounding against my chest. I'm feeling all sorts of things for Sarah. "You are the sexy one."

Sarah places her hand up under my chin while holding my gaze. "I'm going to confess something to you," she says.

"Okay..." My anxiety starts to creep in.

"I've had a thing for you since we first met." She covers her eyes with her hand. I reach out and lower it so I can see her face.

"I can honestly say the same."

"Really?" Sarah seems surprised. "You are a hard person to read."

"I thought I gave it away too many times." I smile, thinking of all the times I let my hand show and can't believe she didn't see it.

"Well." Sarah takes my hand and holds it. "There were moments where I thought you did, then you would pull back and cover yourself. It's been confusing."

"You make me nervous," I admit.

"I do?" Sarah runs her fingers over my hand.

"Yes." I sigh. "You have to know you are like the whole package, right?"

"No. I didn't know that." Sarah smiles broadly with amusement. I feel embarrassed now for admitting that. I'm still buzzed. Maybe that's the reason for being so open in this very exposed moment. I'm not usually so easily affected by the women I've been with. And it's been a long time since I've been with anyone.

"Hey," Sarah says, touching my chin with her finger. "That's the best compliment. Thank you." She kisses me lightly on the lips. "You are captivating. That's the second thought I ever had about you. Beautiful, then captivating."

"You certainly know how to be charming." I smile.

"May I ask you a question?"

"Sure," I say, thinking she could ask me anything at this moment and I'd answer.

"What's the deal with Damon?"

"Oh." I take in a breath and release it. "I have no clue what happened tonight."

"You two haven't…"

"Not at all. He's just a friend. Though I don't know what will happen now." I never expected Damon to try to kiss me. I assumed we were on the same page.

"Have you been with a woman before?" Sarah shifts a little under the covers.

"Yes. I have only ever been with women." The look on Sarah's face tells me that she's relieved with this information. She must have been worried this was my first time with a woman. I've never understood why that's such a big deal anyway. I feel like if you fall in love with the first person you have sex with, and you are together from then on, why can't it work? All relationships take work. Not that I've ever been in one. I've had my hands too full with helping raise the boys to ever consider a relationship. Good thing there has never been someone I've wanted to move forward with. I've been okay with being casual. Until now.

"I thought so," she says. "But I didn't want to assume." Sarah rubs her hand over the bare skin on my side. "Come here," Sarah turns onto her back and holds her arm out for me to lie on her.

I move until my body is flush with hers, resting my head on her chest, up under her chin. "I should probably get going so you can get some rest." I turn just enough to kiss her chest.

"Could you stay the night?" Her arm comes around to hold me close. She slowly rubs my arm up and down. I think about that question. It would be nice to stay and wake up in her arms. I'm just not sure I should. "Please," Sarah whispers. Her left hand tilts my chin upward so she can kiss me. I move into the kiss, turning more onto my stomach to lie half on Sarah's body. "I'd love for you to stay, but if you can't, I'll understand."

"I'll stay," I say, then kiss her again. I'm not quite done with this night yet.

* * *

"Good morning." The voice next to my ear wakes me as soft lips find my shoulder. I stir, opening my eyes to the bright sunshine. I turn toward Sarah, who is sitting on the edge of the bed. Her blue eyes stare into my soul. I'm pretty sure she touched it multiple times in the last twelve hours.

"Morning." My voice is raspy. Sarah kept me up late last night before we eventually fell asleep in each other's arms.

"I'm going to make us breakfast. You can shower if you'd like. Use whatever you want of mine." I notice that she has already showered, her hair slightly damp and wavy. Its natural state. And she has clothes on. That's not fair.

"You're dressed already. You should have woken me." I sit up, pulling the covers to my chest, and run my fingers through my sex hair.

"I," she says with almost a bashful look, "wanted to look nice for you when you woke up." I smile, liking that she did that for me. I love the look in her eyes this morning as she looks at me.

"I would have rather had you next to me," I admit, feeling more open than I have in a long time. She makes me want to do that. For her.

"Aw." Her fingertips trace a line from my shoulder down to my hand. "You're adorable. You looked so peaceful this morning. I enjoyed the sight of you in my bed." She smiles, and I can tell she is genuinely happy I'm here. "Plus." Sarah lifts my hand to her breast. "I'm not completely dressed." She is braless.

I squeeze the softness underneath. "You are full of surprises."

"And you are sexy as hell." Sarah lightly kisses my lips. "Bacon and eggs?" she says, then kisses the side of my neck. "Or blueberry pancakes?" She lowers her mouth to the area above my breast next to the sheet covering me.

"Um…" I tilt my head back, enjoying her lips on me. "My mind is not working right now."

Sarah laughs, her lips still against my skin. "I can't seem to get enough of you."

"I'm not complaining." I love the attention. She is being attentive and soft. I could get used to this.

"I'm glad." She stands. "I'll go get started. If I stay here any longer, I'll end up back in bed with you."

"That's not a bad thing," I say as she walks out of the room. I hear her laugh.

Though Sarah offered me her shower, I decide to wait until I get home. I don't want to stay too long this morning in case she has plans. I get up and look around for my clothes. Sarah has folded them and placed them on the upholstered bench at the foot of the bed. I take my clothes to the bathroom and close the door. I dress quickly, not feeling as confident as I did last night. My hair is wild. I use Sarah's brush, then pull it up in a messy bun. I squeeze some toothpaste onto my finger and run it over my teeth and tongue. I wipe the mascara out from under my eyes so I look more presentable. I look one last time in the mirror. This will have to do. I open the door and smell the bacon cooking. And I think I hear the coffee brewing. I'm feeling an overwhelming sense of happiness. I can't remember the last time I felt this way.

I hear my phone beeping from somewhere in Sarah's room. Looking around for it, I have no clue where it ended up or how it even made it in here. It goes off again, and I spot it on Sarah's dresser. There is a text from Damon. I don't open it. I'm not ready to deal with that right now. My morning is going too well.

The smell of bacon guides me to the kitchen where Sarah is standing at the stove. I stop at the island. I want to go over and wrap my arms around her, but for whatever reason, I'm feeling a bit shy.

"Bacon and eggs?" I ask, sliding onto the barstool.

"Bacon, eggs, and waffles. I think you deserve it after last night." She turns around to smile at me. She looks at my clothes. "I could have let you borrow something more comfortable."

"This is fine," I reassure her. I'm wearing my same denim jeans and gray V-neck shirt from yesterday.

"You do wear it well." She winks at me as she turns back to the stove. I've never had someone wink at me like Sarah does. I love when she does it.

I reach down deep and find my self-confidence to walk over to Sarah and wrap my arms around her waist. She makes me feel like I can do anything. Sarah sighs and snuggles back into me. I rest my chin on her shoulder.

"This is nice," she says.

"Agreed." I squeeze her gently and kiss her neck.

Sarah goes to turn the bacon and it pops. "Ouch," I jump back.

"Did it get you?" She continues to flip the rest of the bacon.

"Just a little." I rub the spot. "I haven't seen anyone cook bacon this way except at cafés. We buy the microwavable kind."

"This is how my mom and grandma does it. It just stuck. I don't buy it that often, but I like to indulge occasionally."

Sarah finishes up the cooking, and we sit down to eat. "This is amazing," I say, then take another bite of the waffles. "Is there something you're not good at?" I tease.

"Plenty, but I can't throw myself under the bus just yet." She smiles.

We finish breakfast while having light conversation. I get up and insist on cleaning up. Though Sarah does a great job of trying to resist my help, I win in the end.

I hear my phone beep again and hope it's not Damon. I dry off my hands and check just to make sure it isn't Mom or the boys. I'm sure I will catch hell for not checking in last night. It's sad to be my age and still get treated in such a way by my mom. I should stand up for myself. One of these days, I will. Maybe after I move out.

The text message is from Brayden asking me where I am. *Be home soon, little man*, I send back. I know he misses me when I'm not there because I show him attention, but I can't stay home all the time.

"Everything okay?" Sarah is looking at me from across the bar.

"Yes." I smile, so she knows I'm telling the truth. "I do need to get back home. Shower, laundry, schoolwork." I shrug.

"Let me finish dressing and I'll take you." She stands.

"No." I lift my hand. "I can just get an Uber. You don't have to go to the trouble. Enjoy your day off."

Sarah walks over to me, resting her hands on my waist. "I would very much enjoy it if you would let me drive you home. Okay?" she says.

"Okay." I nod, then smile because she is so cute that I can't keep it in.

"See that wasn't so hard, was it?" She pecks my lips before rushing off to her bedroom to change.

I sit at the table so I can drink the rest of my orange juice while I wait on Sarah. I decide to bite the bullet and open the message from Damon. *I just want to say that I'm sorry for last night. I had a little too much to drink. I hope you can forgive me.* I don't know what to say back to him. I'm sure we can be friends again, but I need time to process things.

I take my glass to the sink and wash it, dry my hands on the towel hanging from the stove, then pick up my phone. *Thanks for apologizing,* I reply and leave it at that.

CHAPTER SEVENTEEN

Sarah pulls the car to the side of the road a couple blocks from the house. I shift in my seat to face her. "I'm sorry about this. But thank you for understanding."

"Is your mom hard on you about dating women?" Sarah seems a little more reserved now than she was earlier at her house. I get it—we have a lot to learn about each other.

"I've never told her that I'm gay. We don't really talk about my life. She doesn't ever ask." I realize how that may sound to Sarah, but it's the truth and I don't want to lie to her.

"She's never asked why you don't date guys?"

"No. She doesn't know I date at all."

"Oh." Sarah looks down at her hands.

"I keep to myself. I've never introduced anyone ever to my mom. It's hard to when…" I pause, trying to think of how to say this. "She doesn't care."

"I'm sorry." Sarah takes my hand in hers. "You deserve so much more."

"It's all I've ever known." I squeeze her hand. "You are kind of amazing." My heart is full being here with Sarah. She cares about me, and it's not fake.

Sarah smiles. "I had a great time last night and this morning." She leans across the console to kiss me.

"So did I." I smile, looking into those baby blues. I'm about to give Sarah another kiss when out of the corner of my eye I see a car driving by. I look past Sarah's head to meet the driver's stare. I follow her gaze until she passes. "Shit! That was my mom." I feel sick.

"She probably doesn't remember who I am," Sarah says.

"She does. Trust me." I wasn't about to tell Sarah that Mom mentioned her over and over again after the meeting in the principal's office. She said some distasteful things that I would never repeat.

"I'm sorry." Sarah laces her fingers through mine. "Is there anything I can do to help?"

"No." I shake my head and force a smile. "It'll be fine." I know I will get the third degree when I get home, but I'll keep that part to myself. "Thank you for the ride home." I lift Sarah's hand to my lips and kiss the top. She pulls it away and starts the engine. "What are you doing?"

"No sense in walking now. She already knows about us." She pulls out onto the street. I feel anxious knowing she is about to see where I live. The house needs to be power washed and painted. The grass only grows in patches, and that's mostly weeds. I can go on and on, but why keep torturing myself?

"There." I point. "The white house."

Sarah pulls over. I look over to see Sarah looking at me, not my house. "Call me later?" she asks. The furrow of her brows lets me know she is concerned.

"Of course." I force another smile, hoping she can't tell. I grab the handle of the door. "Thank you, Sarah. Be safe going home." I get out so not to linger any longer.

I walk with my head held high. I do not turn around to see if Sarah is watching. I keep my eyes forward and focused, for what lies ahead of me, behind those doors, requires courage.

The front door seems like the best option at trying to miss Mom. Unfortunately, she is sitting at the dining table waiting for me. There is an open bottle of whiskey and a full glass sitting in front of her. Who knows how much she downed before I walked in.

"Who the fuck was that dropping you off down the street? Scared for me to know, huh?" Her eyes are burning a hole in me.

"She's a friend." I look up the stairs, hoping the boys come down soon. She usually isn't as mean to me in front of them.

"I know who she is." She is seething. "Do I have 'dumb shit' written across my forehead or 'born yesterday' stamped on my ass?" She stands and walks over to me.

"No." I look away. I hate that I allow her to intimidate me.

She grabs my chin and yanks my face so that I'm looking her in the eyes. "You been conspiring against me with that damn teacher, haven't you?"

"No, I have no—"

Pop! The slap across my face causes my head to move with the blow.

"Don't fucking lie to me," she spits, yanking my face back to hers. I smell the whiskey on her breath.

"I'm no—"

Pop! My head jerks again with another slap across my face. This time I do stumble with the force.

"Please, stop." My voice breaks.

Mom grabs my arm and yanks me back to her. "Tell me the damn truth, Brynlee. Did I raise a backstabbing asshole? Did you go and team up against me because you think you know what's best for my son? Are you the reason I was called to the school this week?"

"Mom, please. I'm just trying to help Brayden."

The hit from her knuckles causes me to black out for a moment. I'm down on my knees at the bottom of the stairs. Mom's hands are in my hair pulling my head back while she yells at me, her breath warm against my face. I can't make out what she is saying, but I do hear the boys crying. Ben and Brayden are hovering over me now. They are yelling at her to stop.

"Bryn," the boys say. "Are you okay?"

I realize my head fell forward when Mom released my hair. I'm looking down at the stairs, unsure if I'm seeing blood or tears.

"Bryn," they cry.

I lift my arm to pat whoever is closest to me on the leg. "I'm okay, boys," I finally manage.

"You're bleeding," Ben says. "Brayden, run get a washcloth."

I lift my head up when I feel Brayden get up. "I'm okay, Ben. Let me go upstairs to the bathroom." I look over at Mom, who is just standing there staring at me. She looks shocked.

"Mom, why did you do this?" Ben yells at her. "What is wrong with you?"

"I…" Mom says but doesn't finish. She looks back at me one last time before turning to walk away. I hear the back door slam shut.

"Here." Brayden pushes a dish towel in my hand. I press it against my eye, then try to stand. Ben puts his shoulder underneath my arm and helps me up. I feel a little off-balance, but I am determined to be strong. I stand up straight, grab the railing, and take the stairs one at a time.

I feel a little steadier by the time I reach the bathroom. The mirror shows a face I don't want to see. My left cheek is bright red where I was slapped. I lower the dish towel to reveal a small cut on my right eye. It's not too big, but the blood continues to flow out of it.

The boys are standing behind me with tear-streaked faces. I sit down on the commode and motion for them to come to me. They rush over, but then gently walk into my embrace. I hold them in my arms while biting back the tears threatening to spill from my eyes. I clear my throat. "I'm okay, you guys. Promise."

"What happened?" Ben asks, stepping back to arm's length. Brayden is still leaning into me, wiping his fresh tears away.

"Mom saw me with Brayden's teacher. She was upset about it."

Ben shakes his head. "But why did she hit you, Bryn? Why would she do that?"

I don't have an answer for him because I don't understand myself. So, I give him the best answer I can come up with. "She lost her temper, I guess."

"Will she lose her temper again?" Brayden sniffles.

"Never with you and Ben. She loves you too much." I hope that is the truth. I've always known Mom loved them more than me, and I was okay with that. I just never thought she hated me until today.

"We love you." Ben wipes his eyes.

"And I love you. Both of you." I clear my throat again. "So very much."

I stand to look in the mirror again. My tears are getting harder to hold back. I pull the towel down from my eye to see if the blood has stopped yet. It's slowing down.

"Boys," I say, sitting back down. "You know that you both mean the world to me, right?" They nod. A tear slides down my left cheek. "But I have to leave." I swallow down the lump in my throat. Brayden starts crying again. "And it may be a little while before I can see you."

"No!" Brayden yells. "Please don't go, Bryn. Don't leave us." He rushes to me to wrap his arms around my neck. I let him cry while I hold my tears back, for now. I have to power through this for them so they know that I'm okay. That everything will be okay. And I hope in the end it will be. Hope is what I'm holding on to right now.

Ben walks over and puts his arms around both of us. We stay like that for a little while. I don't know when I'll get to see them again after I leave, so I want to hold on to this moment. It will be the first time they have ever been without me. And the first time they will have ever had to depend on just Mom for everything.

"Guys," I say, sliding them to each side of my arms. "I need to go pack some clothes. Want to come to my room with me?" They nod.

I get on my phone to get an Uber on its way. I quickly pack a suitcase of clothes and gather some shoes, my toiletries, and stuff them in the duffel bag. I'll have to come back for the rest when I get a place. I have no idea when or where that will be. I don't even have a plan for tonight.

"Ben, please don't let Mom throw my stuff out. I'll come back for it soon."

"Okay," he says, a frown set on his face. This is not ideal for any of us. He grabs my suitcase to carry it downstairs. I pick up my black duffel and follow him.

My ride will be here in less than five minutes. I stop by the kitchen and grab some paper towels to clean up the blood on the stairs.

"Guys." I motion them to me as I sit on the stairs. I feel like I have no energy. "I hate to leave you here alone, but I have no choice. Ben." I look at him directly. "Text or call Mom when I leave and let her know you need her to come home." Ben nods. "I love you both so much." I take one hand of each of them. "I'm always a phone call away. When I get a place, you both will be my first visitors. We can spend the weekend together."

"Please don't leave," Brayden cries.

"It's time for me to go, little man. I need you to be strong for me. Can you do that?"

He covers he eyes with the bend of his arm. "I'm gonna miss you too much."

I pull them both into one final hug, knowing I need to get up and go. "I will miss you both very much."

"Can we call you tonight?" Ben sniffs.

"Absolutely." My voice breaks, but I smile to play it off.

I stand, grab my bags, and walk to the door before it gets any harder than it is. I put my hand on the doorknob. "I love you," I say without turning around. "Lock this door." I close it quickly, hearing a faint whimper, and then the door lock clicks.

The Uber hasn't arrived yet, but I can wait by the road. It shouldn't be much longer. I stop midway down the walkway when I see Mom sitting in her car. She looks at me. My stomach tightens with all the unshed tears, unsaid words, and unwarranted hate for all the years I've been her daughter. I walk toward her, stopping next to the car. Her window is down. She is smoking a cigarette. She hasn't smoked in years.

"Why do you hate me?" I exhale, finally finding my nerve. "I don't even remember the last time you said anything nice to me, if ever. I've always tried to be a good daughter. I wanted you to love me. To be proud of me. I don't think you are capable of it. So, why? What did I ever do to deserve this?"

Mom blows out a puff of smoke from her cigarette. She reaches down to the middle console and lifts up a couple folded notebook papers. She hands them out the window to me without a word. She doesn't even glance my way. Her eyes stay straight ahead as she takes another drag from her cigarette.

The Uber pulls up to the curb. I look back at the papers in her hand, confused by what they are. I take them, fold them twice over, and shove them into my back pocket. "I'll be back to get the rest of my stuff soon," I say as I walk away.

The driver pops the trunk and I put my things in the back. I get into the back seat and look up toward the house one last time. Ben and Brayden are standing at the window staring at me. My heart aches at the sight as we drive away.

* * *

I get a cheap hotel room near my work. That way, I can easily walk. Unpacking my suitcase should be a mindless job, but I'm all over the place. I feel empty inside. I take my personal items to the bathroom, get out some clothes and hang them in the closet because I'll be here a while, then I just put the others on the other bed. I don't want to do anything else. I grab my phone and sit on the floor at the end of the bed. I dial Andrea. It rings twice before she answers.

"Hey, hey, what's my favorite girl doin'?"

Any other time I would smile. My face hurts to do anything. "Andrea," I manage, before the tears flow hard down my face and a sob escapes my lips.

"Bryn, what's wrong?" Andrea is frantic. "Are you injured? Talk to me."

"I'm—" I sob again, trying to get the words out, but feeling too heartbroken.

"You're scaring me," Andrea says. "Please, Bryn."

I take in a deep breath and release it. Closing my eyes, I lift my chin toward the ceiling to try to calm myself. "I'm sorry." I sniff. "I'm okay."

"I've got my keys in my hand. I'm coming to you." Andrea's voice sounds shaky. She's never heard me cry. I'm very private with my emotions. "Where are you?"

"I'm okay. Really. I'm not home. I left." I keep my sobs at bay, and only the tears fall from my eyes effortlessly as I tell my story of how my mom hit me. I leave no detail out. I normally downplay things so my mom doesn't look so bad. Not this time. I tell it all. When I'm done, I hear Andrea sniffle on her end.

"I'm so sorry. I can't imagine any mother ever doing that to their own child, much less you, my kindhearted, selfless friend." Her words are comforting. "I'm coming to get you. You are staying with me and baby girl. As long as I have a home, you have a home."

I grab a tissue from the dresser. "That means more to me than you could ever imagine, but right now I just need to be alone."

"You *need* your best friend."

"I'll always need my best friend," I agree. I don't want her to see this as a rejection. "But tonight, I'm not going to be worth being around." Plus, I am embarrassed for anyone to see how I look right now. It's one thing to say what happened. It's another to show the evidence.

"I don't care if you lounge on my couch all week with blackout curtains and eat ramen noodles or cereal while watching QVC, as long as you are here with me."

I want to smile at that, but my body and mind can't make the effort. I'm beyond exhausted. "I can't, Andrea." I wipe my face again. "Please just understand. I'm going to go now. I need to lie down for a bit."

Andrea sighs loudly. She hates giving in. "I'm not happy about this," she says.

"I know."

"I'll call you in a little bit and talk some sense into you."

"Okay," I say weakly.

"Hugs," she says.

"Hugs." I hang up, then climb up on the bed. I rest my tired eyes. I just need a moment to lie here and not think.

CHAPTER EIGHTEEN

The faint sound of my phone vibrating wakes me from my sleep. The insistent noise was even in my dreams. Or so I thought. I squint at my phone. My eyelids feel puffy from all the tears. I have ten messages and five missed calls from Andrea. Sarah has texted and called me as well. I must have been asleep for a while. I try to focus on the numbers. Eight o'clock. Wow, I was tired.

I scroll through Andrea's messages first, which start out fine, but by the last one she is in hysterics. Something about her not thinking clearly and I probably shouldn't have laid down since I took a blow to the head. A little too late now. I'm about to text her back, without reading Sarah's messages, but a new text comes in from Sarah.

Where are you? Sarah says. *Andrea and I are both worried. Either answer this text or I'm going to call the police to help us find you.*

Yikes. I swiftly type out a text, trying to avoid that disaster. *I'm at a hotel. I was asleep. Sorry.*

Which one? Sarah messages me back. *And what room?*

I send a quick reply answering her questions and then wait for her response. Nothing comes back right away. I lie back down on the bed again and close my eyes. I'm still so tired.

Knock, knock, knock. "Brynlee, it's me. Open up."

I sit up, startled. Is that Sarah? Am I awake?

"Bryn, please," she says again. She must have been driving around.

I slowly get up, unsure of my legs at this point, and run my hand through my hair. When I open the door, Sarah is standing there with her arms crossed, brows furrowed, and yet she is still beautiful as ever.

"May I come in?" she asks, her blue eyes deep with concern.

"Yeah, sorry." I step to the side, allowing her to enter.

She walks around the room, looking at my new living arrangements. I adjust my hair over the corner of my right eye to cover the cut. I haven't even taken the time to clean it. I'm sure I look awful with dried blood on my face. I haven't showered either. I don't want her to see me like this; that's why I didn't call her. That, and I'm embarrassed that any of this happened to begin with. I bet Sarah's family is kind and respectful. I bet her mom would never hit her.

Sarah starts gathering my clothes and putting them in my suitcase. I'm confused. She folds a shirt, then jeans, and stacks them inside.

"What are you doing?"

She glances at me but keeps packing. "I'm taking you to my house."

I walk over and place my hand over hers in the open suitcase of clothes. "Please, don't." It comes out as soft as a whisper.

Sarah puts her other hand over mine and squeezes. "It hurt enough already that you didn't call me, and I had to find out from Andrea, so please don't do this."

"How?" I'm lost. Andrea contacted her without having her number.

"Facebook." Sarah takes a deep breath and releases it. "Look maybe what we shared last night didn't mean as much to you as it did to me, and that's okay, but—"

"Sarah." I interrupt because that's not at all how I feel.

"Please let me finish." She holds up her hand. "I have a big house that I live in alone. You can stay in the guest room, above the garage, wherever you are comfortable. You do not have to stay in my bedroom. But please, Brynlee, come home with me. My heart has been run through the mud today, and I just want to help the person I care about tonight or as long as you will let me."

My eyes fill with tears even though I try hard to stop them. They spill out onto my cheeks. I don't sob. I don't make a noise. I am the one who is always looking out for others. I've never had someone do that for me. Until Andrea, I never let anyone get close. It was just me and the boys.

Sarah pulls me into her arms. I don't have the words to thank her right now. She holds me tight. I wrap my arms around her waist. I cry harder now. I let all my emotions out. Sarah strokes the back of my head, then rubs my back and kisses the side of my face multiple times, all while whispering words of comfort.

"I'm sorry," I say, wiping at the shoulder of her shirt, which is now covered in my tears.

"I'm not worried about that." She pushes the hair over my right eye behind my ear to reveal my cut. She brushes the back of her fingers down my cheek. "Let's get you home. You can shower and I can clean that up."

Sarah goes back to putting my things into the suitcase. I get all my stuff from the bathroom and put it back in the duffel bag. When everything is packed, I follow Sarah out the door and into her car. She stops under the check-in awning at the front desk and runs the keys back inside. I wait in the car.

"They are only going to charge you for tonight," Sarah says as she slides back into the driver's seat. She buckles her seat belt. "They'll give you a refund for the rest of the week." She shakes her head in what seems like disappointment.

"Thank you." I turn my head to look out the window. Her disappointment in me hurts.

Sarah and I ride in silence. Her hand on my leg, and my hand on top of hers. That's exactly what I need. I know she is hurt that I didn't call after we shared such a special night, but this is my mess to deal with. My family problems. I had no clue Sarah would even want me to call her with my problems. It isn't like we have talked about what to expect from each other. We are kind of just stumbling through this as we go. But now that I know how she feels about this, I'm willing to be more open. I want to be that for her. She came to my rescue when I didn't even know I needed it.

It takes no time at all and we are pulling into the garage at Sarah's house. She pops the trunk. The suitcase is closest to me, so I grab it. Sarah reaches in and lifts out the duffel bag. We enter the house from the garage into the kitchen. Sarah drops her keys on the table and leads me down the hall toward the bedrooms. She stops at the bottom of the stairs. Her bedroom is straight ahead. The guest rooms are upstairs. She turns.

"Is my room okay to shower in?" She looks almost hurt. She has no clue how much she means to me already. "If not, the guest bath is just here." She points to her left. "And there's one upstairs."

"Your room is good. If that's okay." I say that because of how unsure she looks. I choose it because if she wants to share her room with me, then that's exactly where I want to be.

"Absolutely." She continues down the hall and into her bedroom. She places my duffel on the bench at the end of the bed. I stand there, feeling out of place. I can't snap out of the mood I'm in, even though I am thankful for all she is doing for me.

"Thank you," I say, and I know I should give more, but I don't know how.

Sarah nods. "Have you eaten anything since you left here this morning?"

"No." I shake my head. I haven't even thought about food until she mentioned it. Now that I'm reminded of it, my stomach does feel a little achy.

"I'll make you something while you shower. Do you have a preference?"

I cross my arms, feeling vulnerable in the moment. "I'm not picky."

Sarah walks to up to me and rubs the upper part of my arms as if she can read what's going on inside me. "It's going to be okay," she says, touching the side of my face. "Come to the living room when you're done. Okay?"

"Okay." I watch Sarah walk out and close the door behind her. I appreciate that she is giving me some privacy to clean up.

I look around at the familiar bedroom from this morning. I didn't think I'd be back so soon. Especially not this way. How quickly life can change in an instant.

Before I do anything else, I grab my phone and type a quick text to Andrea. *I'm at Sarah's now. She came to get me at the hotel. I'm doing okay. Going to shower and eat dinner. Call you tomorrow.*

I put my suitcase in the corner of the room, out of the way, and find some clothes for after the shower. I place them on the end of the bed. I gather my toiletries and walk into the bathroom. The bathtub is in the middle of the room against the back wall and underneath the window. A standup shower is in the corner. It's a nice big one with glass sides and no door. I turn the water on and let the hot water run while I undress. I feel sore, like I've been in a wreck or something.

The water feels so good when I step into the shower. The hot water runs over my head and face, then my neck and shoulders. It is wonderful. After I wash my hair and body, I turn off the nozzle and get out. I have no clue how long I've been in here. The room is steamy. I towel dry off, wrap my hair, then slip into my clothes. I take a brush from my bag and run it through my thick hair. I can let it air dry, but I decide it's best to blow dry instead. About three-fourths of the way through drying it, I shut it off. It can finish drying on its own now.

I lean closer to the mirror to inspect my eye. It's red and a little swollen, but it doesn't look too bad. It's the first time I've ever been hit. It doesn't feel real.

I open the door from Sarah's room and walk down the hall to find her sitting on the couch. "Hi," I say, feeling awkward in my surroundings.

"Hey," she says, then smiles softly as if she is happy to finally see me. "How was the shower?"

"Great, actually." I walk toward her and see first aid supplies on her coffee table.

"I have tomato soup on low and I waited for you to make the grilled cheese. Does that sound okay? If not, I can make something else."

My heart is all over the place today with being crushed, stomped, and beaten down, but now I feel happy. I need happy.

"That sounds good. Thank you." I walk over to sit next to her on the sofa. She has the television on but the volume low. It's my favorite movie, *You've Got Mail*. "I love this movie."

"Me too." She scoots closer to me. "May I look at your eye?"

"Sure." That ashamed feeling creeps back up. I know this isn't my fault. I know I'm not to blame, but it doesn't make it any less embarrassing. I need to keep in mind that people all over the world have it harder than I do.

Sarah reaches behind her and turns on another lamp. I'm glad she leaves the overhead light off. She moves my hair behind my ear so it's out of the way. I watch as she gently touches my eye. "I think this will heal up just fine. But we should use ointment, so it doesn't scar."

"Okay." I haven't taken care of it at all since it happened. But I really don't want a scar right there on my face.

Sarah takes a Q-tip with some ointment on it and runs it over my cut. I twitch at the contact. "Oh, baby. I'm sorry." She touches my cheek before continuing. That's the first time she has used a term of endearment. It surprises me so much that I hold on to that warm feeling as she works on my eye.

When Sarah finishes applying a bandage over my cut at the corner of my eyebrow, she lets her hand glide down my cheek, runs it behind my head and into my hair. Her soft lips press against mine in a light kiss. She whispers against my lips, "I'm so sorry this happened to you." I close my eyes, feeling her hurt within me. While I am emotionally restrained, she wears her heart on her sleeve. She wraps her arms around me, pulling me closer for a hug. I squeeze her back, burying my head in her hair.

It's the best hug I've ever received. She holds me for a long time before breaking away.

"Let me make your grilled cheese," she says, standing. "Here." She hands me the remote from the coffee table. "Relax, please. I'll be right back with your dinner."

I lean back on the couch and turn the volume up. I feel a tear leak from the corner of my eye. I wipe it quickly, so Sarah doesn't see. I don't remember the last time I cried so much. The tears are a mix of heartbreak caused by Mom, missing the boys, and an overwhelming feeling I have for Sarah. I'm not sure how I got so lucky or what I did to deserve to meet someone as special as her, but I hope this is the beginning of a long relationship. I think when you know, you just know. Why do you need years to figure out when someone is perfect for you? I didn't believe it could happen until now.

I smell the food before I see it. Sarah slides a tray onto my lap. "Dinner is served," she says. I almost argue that I can eat in the kitchen, but I stop because she made the effort to make me comfortable.

"Thank you." I smile. "It smells really good."

"What would you like to drink?"

"Water, please."

The first spoonful of creamy tomato soup is delicious. I make myself go slow so as not to look uncivilized. I dip the corner of the grilled cheese into the soup and take a bite. I close my eyes as I chew.

"That good, huh?" Sarah smiles as she places the glass of water next to me.

"I didn't realize how hungry I was." I take another spoonful of soup.

"It's been at least twelve hours since you last ate," Sarah says as she sits down next to me.

"Very true." I look at the clock above the fireplace. It's almost ten o'clock. I've never skipped a meal before. But I also have never been punched in the face by my mother.

"My dad dips his grilled cheese in his soup too." Sarah grins.

"Doesn't everybody?" I dip again and finish that side of the sandwich.

"I don't like my bread soggy." She chuckles.

I laugh, then wince a little. My jaw is sore. "But your bread gets soggy as soon as it gets inside your mouth."

"I'm weird." Sarah lifts one shoulder and lets it fall. She leans back onto the couch next to me. She turns up the volume to the television. I finish my soup and finish off the glass of water. I take it to the kitchen and wash the dishes.

When I get back to the couch, Sarah has a blanket pulled over her lap. "Come here." She lifts the blanket and I slide in next to her. She covers us both up, then loops her arm around mine to hold my hand. I rest my head on her shoulder as we watch the rest of the movie. My eyes feel heavy again.

"Brynlee," Sarah says, her hand running through my hair. "Let's go to bed."

I open my eyes to see the ending credits roll across the screen on the TV. Sarah picks up the remote and clicks it off. She offers me her hand, helping me up. She switches off the lamps on the way to the bedroom as we walk hand in hand.

The light next to Sarah's bed is still on from when I showered. We both go to the bathroom to brush our teeth. I have mine laid on the side of the sink. When we finish, Sarah instructs me to put it in the toothbrush holder next to hers.

Sarah stops on the left side of the bed and removes her bra and pants. She climbs into bed wearing only her T-shirt. I do the same and get in on the other side. She turns off the lamp and we lay on our pillows face-to-face.

My eyes are finally adjusting to the darkness so I can see more of Sarah's features. "I don't know how to ever repay you for being so good to me. And I mean straight back to the very beginning when we met."

"You can repay me by taking care of yourself, finishing school, and continuing to be you. I've never met anyone like you before." Sarah places her hand on top of my forearm that is partially tucked under my pillow.

I move over to her, taking her cheek in my hand and kissing her. Not gently, not rough, but as passionately as I can. She reciprocates, sliding her tongue against mine. I break away long enough to pull my shirt over my head. She does the same, then takes off her underwear. I do as well. I position myself on top of her, our breasts pushed against each other. We both gasp with the contact. I kiss her again.

"Are you sure?" she asks, pulling her head away from me to look me in the eyes. "We don't have to. We can just sleep."

"I want to. More than anything." I lower my lips to hers again. She clearly accepts that answer as her hands find my ass and pull me closer against her. We move together perfectly until we are both wet. I sit up and straddle her, rubbing our centers against each other. Her breath hitches with each move. My hand is on her breast, her hand on my thigh. I go faster, then reach behind me and enter her as I continue rubbing against her, matching our rhythms together. She comes fast and hard. She squeezes her legs against me, and I go over the top with her.

I thought I was done until she pushes her fingers between us and inside me and I ride out another wave on top of her. I fall next to her, onto my back. She rolls over to lie on my chest, wrapping her arm around my waist. She kisses my cheek. We hold each other without words. I look up at the ceiling as she snuggles me close. I feel tears coming out again. What the hell is wrong with me? I want to wipe them, but then Sarah would know. So, I let them fall down my cheek and hope she doesn't notice.

"Are you okay, baby?" Sarah pushes up just a little to look at me. "Did I hurt you anywhere?" She wipes my cheek. Guess I wasn't very secretive after all.

"I'm okay. I think it's just a lot of emotions for me today. I've honestly never cried so much. I'm sorry." I wipe my other cheek. I'm so annoyed with myself.

"Don't ever apologize for that," Sarah says. "It's good to let it out. I was just afraid that it was me that caused it."

"You did, in a way." I look her in the eyes. "I'm really happy right now. It doesn't seem real." I swipe at my face again.

Sarah kisses me. "You deserve to be happy." She lies back down with her head on my chest and holds me tight. Her leg pushes between mine. "You make me happy too."

We lie like that for a good while. I feel Sarah's breathing get slower, so I know she has fallen asleep. For some odd reason,

I'm wide awake. "I love you," I whisper so low that no one could hear. Then I kiss the top of her head. I've never felt this way for anyone else before. I'm too afraid to tell Sarah while she is awake. I don't want her to say that it is too soon, or any other reason there could be. I know what I feel in my heart, and it's beyond the physical.

I watch the ceiling fan spin until my eyes get too heavy to keep open. Tomorrow is another day to start fresh.

CHAPTER NINETEEN

The sun shining through the windows wakes me. The blinds are closed, but it's still bright. I slept hard. I'm lying on my side, Sarah's arm is draped across my waist, and her naked body is flush to mine. I take her hand and hold it against my chest.

"Good morning," Sarah kisses the back of my shoulder.

"Morning," I say in my sleepy voice. I turn to lie on my back.

Sarah props up on her arm, her hair falling around her shoulders and across the tops of her breasts meeting the blanket that's covering the rest of her. "Messy hair." She runs her hand through it. "But I slept in with you." She smiles shyly. It's adorable.

"You're beautiful." And I truly mean it. "I'm glad you slept in with me."

She smiles, her eyes bright blue from the sun shining on her face. "As long as you don't run away frightened." She grins.

"Never." I smile.

"Your eye looks puffy today." She runs her fingertip near the surrounding skin. "How does it feel?"

I wiggle my eyebrow to check the soreness and Sarah chuckles at me. "It's not too bad." It still hurts, but I don't want to think about it anymore.

"I'm glad," Sarah says. "How about coffee and cinnamon rolls for breakfast?"

"That sounds perfect."

Sarah pushes the covers back and slides out of bed. She walks naked toward the bathroom, confidently at that. I stare in awe of her perfect body.

"You are sexy," I say.

She stops in the doorway of the bathroom and tosses her head over her shoulder. Her long blond hair is tousled, and I love it. "No. That's you, sweetheart," she says. "Trust me on that." Sarah disappears into the bathroom.

The way she makes my insides jump is a wonderful feeling. I'm sure she knows what she is doing to me. I go to my suitcase and get some clothes out. I stand next to the bed and slip on a pair of joggers and a T-shirt.

When I look up, Sarah is standing at the sink washing her hands. She's wearing a robe that only comes to mid-thigh. I watch as she dries her hands, then brushes her hair. I can't believe I am here in her room again. Things have changed dramatically in two days.

"Honestly," I say, walking up behind Sarah. "I've never seen anyone look as gorgeous as you in the morning."

Sarah looks at me through the mirror. "You are the charmer." She turns and steps into my arms. "I think I'll keep you." She presses her lips to mine.

"That's a good thing, considering you kicked me out of the hotel." I tickle her sides. She squirms out of my grip.

"My bed missed you." She grins as she walks away, leaving me in the bathroom.

"Just your bed?" A smile eases across my face.

Sarah turns at the bedroom door and gives me the sexiest look. "You know the answer to that." She winks and walks down the hall, leaving me to stare at the sway of her hips. I do love when she winks at me with those amazing eyes.

I brush my hair and teeth, then gather my clothes from last night. I put them beside the suitcase on the floor. I see the letter from my mom hanging out of the back pocket of my jeans. I take it out and shove it into the side of my suitcase. I left my phone uncharged last night. I still have fifteen percent somehow. Ben and Brayden didn't call or message. That hurts.

I read the message from Andrea asking me to call today. The charger is still in my duffel. I shuffle through the things to find it, then plug in my phone so I can call her later.

Today is already better than last night. I'm a little more relaxed than I expected. I slip on a pair of socks, then head to the kitchen to spend the morning with an incredible woman who makes me feel like I matter.

* * *

"I was so worried about you," Andrea says for the second time since I got in her car. "Don't ever do me like that again."

"I'm sorry," I say, yet again. I've already told her that my phone was on vibrate from when I was out at the bar, so there was no way I could have heard it ring while I was asleep. And I was sleeping hard.

Andrea and I are headed to get lunch. She called this morning begging to get together. I agreed. After I told Sarah of my plans, she decided to go and visit her grandmother. Before I left, she handed me a spare key to the house. I was surprised by the action, and also warmed by the thought.

"I'm sorry I contacted Sarah on Facebook and got her involved. I didn't know what else to do. I needed reinforcements when I couldn't get hold of you." Andrea looks over at me from the driver's seat. I know she cares about me and wouldn't hurt me in any way. I understand her reasoning.

"It's okay. It worked out."

Andrea turns down 5th Avenue and backs into a parking space. "Although, I am a little hurt you chose Sarah's house over mine." She cocks her head to the side and raises one brow in that sassy way she does.

I smile. "She's more into snuggling than you."

Andrea laughs. "Get out of the car."

I do get out, and so does she. We walk into Uncle Ira's Burger Joint. There is a booth open at the front window, so Andrea asks for that seat.

"Why didn't you bring Aimee?" I ask after the waitress leaves us to look over the menu.

"'Cause you and I need some serious talk time. And baby girl needed to visit her grandparents today. She's been too hyper lately."

"Well, tell her I miss her, and that you are mean for not letting her come." I cut my eyes over the top of the menu toward Andrea because I know that will ruffle her feathers.

"Don't play," she says, clicking her tongue and giving me a straight-faced look.

I chuckle. I love the way she lightens my mood. I've never had a close friend until Andrea. Even in high school I was reserved. I wasn't allowed to do anything with a friend because I had to look after Ben and Brayden. Mom was always picking up extra shifts or laying out at the bar looking for her next loser. There was no time for me to have a close friend.

The waitress comes back with the two waters and gets our food order. I don't know why I looked at the menu—I knew what I would get before we walked in. They have the best burgers anywhere around. They use real hamburger meat, patted out themselves, and seasoned on a toasted bun.

"Have you talked to your mom or the boys?" Andrea dives right in.

"No." I shake my head. "The boys said they would call last night but they didn't. I imagine she took their phones."

Andrea wrinkles her forehead with a look of disgust. "I am in shock about this whole thing."

"Try being me."

"I'd love to have a few words with your mother. I don't give a damn how big she is. I'd be like, pop, pop, pop." Andrea smacks the back of her hand against the other three times "Now hit my girl again."

I smile, though honestly, I'd rather not relive any of it. It was hard enough the first time. "I do have this." I pull the letter from my back pocket to show Andrea. I grabbed it from the suitcase while I was getting dressed.

"What's that?" she asks.

"Apparently, Mom wrote me a letter. I thought she had left after…well, you know. But she was out in the car smoking. She gave it to me when I was leaving."

"What does it say?"

"No clue." I slip it back into my pocket. "I haven't read it."

"What in the world are you waiting for?"

"I guess I'm afraid of what it will say." I take a sip of water. My jaw is tender as well as my eye. There is some bruising around the cut, but I have my hair pulled across my eye to cover most of it.

"Let's read it now." She sticks her hand out toward me. "Come on. Let's get this over with."

I shake my head. "Not right now. I kind of want to be alone when I read it."

Andrea pulls back, her eyebrows creased together. She looks hurt. "Okay. If that's what you want."

"I'm sorry." I sigh. "I just think I need time to process all that has happened. It's a lot."

"You're right." Andrea blows out a breath. "I shouldn't push you. I'm just trying to help."

"And you are. Being here for me means so much. Also eating a big juicy burger and crinkle fries are best friend requirements."

"Oh, I've got that covered."

"I know you do." I smile.

We spend the next couple hours chatting about all sorts of things, leaving out the topic of my mother. One of the main topics is Sarah. I tell her how kind, thoughtful, and comforting she has been. And the chemistry between us is amazing. I also fill her in on the disaster the other night with Damon. Then we split a dessert before parting ways. Andrea begs to take me back to Sarah's. I refuse. I decide to take a walk down to the park. I want a little alone time. I have a letter burning through the pocket of my jeans. Andrea is right; I should read it and be done. Mom has never written me a letter, so maybe that's why I'm a little scared of what it will say.

The pond in the middle of the park is low right now. It hasn't rained as much as it usually does. I sit on the bench in the grassy area overlooking the pond. Trees are scattered around. Ducks are scurrying by, checking to see if I have food for them. I sit directly in the sun, which feels wonderful on my face, but the breeze is chilly. I zip up my jacket to help keep me warm.

I sit for a long moment, looking out at the beautiful scenery. Joggers go by, as well as people out for a stroll with their dogs. I take in a deep breath and release it slowly. I do that a couple more times before reaching in my pocket and pulling out the paper. It's folded into four squares. I steadily open it up until I see the first words. My heart clenches with apprehension of what lies within the lines.

The least I can do is finally give you the truth. Especially after everything that has happened today. I honestly don't mean to hurt you. But I can't seem to stop when my temper flares up with you. You have his eyes. The truth is that I am not your mother. I met your dad when you were just a few months old. Your mother died during childbirth. Your dad was all alone. He didn't have anyone to help him. I guess you could say he was looking for a mother for you when he found me. I didn't realize that was his plan. He fooled me in to believing he loved me. A month after we met, we moved in together. Two months after that I come home from getting groceries and he was gone. He only took his clothes. Left a thousand dollars, a note, and you. The note said that he couldn't do this anymore, and that he hopes I can love you as my own. I was devastated. I was angry. I didn't sign up to raise a kid alone, much less someone else's. You cried all the time after he left. You didn't know me. I couldn't bond with you. I felt so much disgust for your dad. He used me and I despised him for that. I tried my best to take care of you. Maybe I should have given you up for adoption after he left or called the authorities. But for the longest time I thought he'd come back for you. For me. I knew I should tell you the truth about all of this, but you love the boys so much I didn't want you to see them differently. I won't tell them you are not their sister until they are older. But now, at least, you can move on with your life and have a little more knowledge of why things are this way between us. If someone is to blame for all this, it's your father.

She didn't sign the letter. Didn't address it to me. It started, and then it ended.

I look out across the pond at the trees blowing in the wind. I feel numb inside. Five minutes ago, I had a mother. One who was cruel to me, but I had one. No wonder she never showed me any affection. She is incapable of loving me the way she loves the boys. I wish she had never written the letter or that I had never read it. The truth is that the only person who may have ever wanted me died bringing me into this world.

I fold the letter and put it back in my pocket. I stare out ahead of me, not really focusing on anything in particular. I've never felt so alone in all my life as I do right now.

The breeze picks up and lifts my hair lightly from my shoulders. I cross my arms as I shiver, unsure if it's from the chill in the air or the chill in my life.

I'm not sure how long I sit like this. I lose track of time as I watch people scurry by, completely happy and unaffected by my heartache. The sun lowers in the sky, painting a beautiful picture. Ordinarily I would be in awe of this sight, but I can't seem to muster up any feeling. Things seem so wrong. I'm not quite sure how to put into words the emptiness inside of me right now. The letter cut me open, yet I'm not bleeding.

I reach for my phone to check the time. But after a quick body search, I realize I don't have it. A heavy sigh escapes my lips. It's in the console of Andrea's car. I thought she'd be taking me back home, so I left it there. I didn't plan on coming out here to the park. It's too late to worry about that now. I lean back against the bench and watch the world go by. I'm in no hurry to move from this spot anyway. Time stands still for no one, but for me, I'm stuck in this moment of uncertainty, my mind on repeat.

CHAPTER TWENTY

"Where have you been?" Andrea says as she yanks open the door. "I've been looking for you everywhere?"

I'm standing on the front stoop outside her house. I finally made the effort to move from the park and walk all the way here, not caring how long it took, welcoming the burn in my legs. "I was in the park. You have my phone." I shiver.

"I know! I called it." Andrea pulls me into her house. "Get in here. It's cold outside. Have you lost your mind?"

"Possibly." I shiver again. The temperature must be the lowest it's been up to this point. "I need my phone so I can get back to Sarah's."

"Really? That's all you have to say about being gone all damn evening? You have to stop making a habit out of worrying me." Andrea wraps her arms around me and holds me tight. I keep my arms crossed, not really wanting to be comforted in the moment.

"I'm not trying to worry you. I didn't mean to leave my phone."

Andrea drops her arms. "Talk to me. What's going on?"

I inhale, filling my lungs with a deep breath of air before releasing it. "I really just want to get back and take a warm bath."

"Why are you being so closed off with me? Did I do something?"

"No. Please, it's not you. I just don't want to think about anything right now." I want to stay numb. I miss the boys so much it hurts. I miss my bed. I miss being in the dark of all the secrets.

Andrea sighs. "Well, I'm driving you there. And before we leave you are going to eat. I cooked your favorite: chicken and dumplings, green beans, and mashed potatoes. Baby girl would love to see you too." Andrea walks away without waiting for my reply. "Baby girl," she calls out. "Brynlee is here to see you." She looks over her shoulder at me with a satisfied look.

Aimee runs down the hall and jumps in my arms. I lift her up and give her a tight hug. Andrea knows what she is doing. I'm a sucker for Aimee.

"Did you come to color with me?" Aimee asks.

"I'm going to eat some of your mom's yummy food. Will you sit beside me and color me a picture?"

"Yes!" Aimee nods vigorously. I lower her to the floor, and she runs off. I imagine it's to get her coloring supplies.

When I get to the kitchen, Andrea has made me a plate warming in the microwave.

"Sit." She points.

"You're bossy."

"Are you just figuring this out?" Andrea takes my plate from the microwave and slides it onto the table.

"No." I sit down. "Just thought I would remind you."

Andrea opens the refrigerator and pulls out two beers. She unscrews the tops and places one in front of me. "I have an eight-year-old. I'm reminded daily."

Aimee, as if being summoned, barrels down the hall sounding like a wild animal, and into the kitchen where she hops up on a chair beside me. "Which picture do you want?" She flips through the Disney princess coloring book.

"Whichever is your favorite. That's the one I want." I take a bite of the food Andrea gave me. I'm not really hungry, but I should eat.

"Um…" Aimee props her chin on her hand as she searches through the book. "How about Rapunzel? You both have green eyes and at the end of the movie her hair is brown. I could color it brown now, so you are the same."

"I love that idea. Can I take it home with me?"

Aimee smiles big and nods as she pulls out her crayons.

I look over at Andrea, who looks smug knowing she had a hand in keeping me here for dinner. I have to give her credit. She did help ease my troubles for a split second, but my new reality is still there marinating in the back of my mind.

After I finish eating, Andrea and Aimee drive me to Sarah's. I'm surprised that I haven't heard from her at all today. She must have been busy with her family.

"Thanks for the ride," I say as Andrea pulls in Sarah's driveway.

"You're welcome, bestie." Andrea puts the car in park. "Damn, this house is nice. Teachers must make more than I thought."

"Maybe so." I hadn't really thought much on that. "Baby girl." I motion to her. "Come give me a bye hug." She unbuckles her seat belt and wraps her arms around the back of my neck. "You give the best hugs," I say. She giggles as she hops back into her seat.

"I'll see you at work tomorrow." Andrea unlocks the doors for me to get out.

"Yep." I reach down and grab my bag from the floorboard. Andrea stopped by the liquor store for me on the way home. I close the door and give one last wave as I head up the walkway.

The front porch light comes on as I approach the steps. I take out my key to unlock the door. I have no clue if Sarah is home. The foyer lamp is on, but the rest of the house looks dark. When I reach the area between the kitchen and living room, I quickly see that I'm here alone. I pull out my phone to see if there is a message from Sarah. Still nothing.

I pull the bottle of caramel whiskey from the brown bag and place it on the counter. I've had this before and it was great. And I need great tonight. The quiet house feels as empty as I do. It's actually very fitting.

There must be some cocktail glasses somewhere around here. I search through the cabinets until I find a whiskey glass. I pour a hefty amount into the glass, then open the fridge to see what she has for a mixer. Ginger ale works nicely. I pour an equal amount of soda in my glass and then drop in a couple ice cubes to top it off. The first sip is strong, but perfect.

Glass in hand, I head toward Sarah's bedroom for a bath. My legs could use the relaxation from my five-mile walk to Andrea's earlier. I'm used to walking, just not in the shoes I wore today.

I don't turn any lights on throughout the house. The darkness feels good. I do, however, turn on the accent light in the bathroom for my bath. I run the water, take another big sip of my drink, and leave it to find some clothes.

My suitcase—that had been in the corner—is gone. That's weird. So is the duffel bag I had on the bench. I look around the room, unsure of where they are. I feel a little lost in a house that is not my home. I really don't belong anywhere. I walk down the hall and up the stairs so I can check in both guest rooms, hoping something turns up, but also worried Sarah may have moved me out of her room. Upon inspection, I find nothing of mine. I go back to Sarah's room and peek in her huge walk-in closet. My bags are in the back corner. And they are empty. Where are my clothes? I do a quick scan of the closet and see a few of my things hanging in a section that looks newly cleared for me. I'm not sure where the rest of my clothes are, so I'll have to wait until she gets home to find out. Her drawers are not for me to go through.

I go back to the bathroom to check my bath. As I pass by the sink, I see my toiletries. She's made a place for all of my things. I go to the shower and find my shampoo, conditioner, bodywash, and razor. She's been busy while I was out.

I turn off the water, take a couple more swallows of my whiskey cocktail, then strip and get in the bath. The water is hot. It feels nice. I pull my hair up in a clip and relax back, sliding down into the water. I don't remember the last time I had an actual bath.

My mind betrays me as the words in the letter enter my mind. Tears well up with the thought of the woman who raised me, the woman I still feel like is my mother, didn't want me. She probably never even loved me. No wonder I've never heard her say those words to me. It hurts so bad. My chest tightens with each breath I take. My brothers are not biologically kin to me. My dad didn't want me. I was his only link to the woman who gave birth to me, and he pawned me off on someone who doesn't even like me.

My eyes cloud with unshed tears. My whole life has been a lie. I sob into my whiskey glass as I take another drink. I urge it to help me feel numb again. I wish to not feel anything right now. I want this feeling to go away.

I sit up, wash off, and get out. My drink is empty. I towel off my body, let my hair down, and wrap the towel around me before heading to the kitchen for a refill.

The faint sound of a door opening catches my attention. I hear footsteps coming toward me. While I adore Sarah, I don't want her to see me crying again.

"Brynlee?" Sarah's voice comes from behind me. "Hi, I didn't think you were home."

I keep my back to her as I pour another drink. "I haven't been here long." My voice cracks, and I can tell Sarah notices as her footsteps bring her closer.

"Is everything okay?" she asks, her hand resting on my upper bare back.

I keep my eyes downward and my head from her view so that she doesn't see my face. "Yeah. I can't find my clothes." I cross my arms over my chest, feeling vulnerable and exposed.

Sarah removes her hand from my back. I immediately regret how I'm acting toward her, yet I can't seem to change my body language or mood.

"I made room in my dresser on the right side. I hope it's okay that I put them away." Her voice sounds strained. "I should have asked first."

"Thank you." I pick up my drink. "I'll go get dressed." I keep my eyes averted as I leave the kitchen. I feel Sarah watching me, but I don't turn around to check. When I reach her room, I don't close the door while I change. It feels odd doing so. This isn't my room. While Sarah is trying to help me feel comfortable, I can't get out of my own mind and insecurities to allow the possibility of someone actually caring for me. At any moment Sarah could ask me to leave. She could decide I'm too young, this is too soon. I have nothing to offer her. Why would anyone settle for me?

I slip on some comfortable clothes, then fold my dirty ones and lay them beside the laundry basket so I can wash them soon. God, I'm being so weird about everything and I don't know how to change it. I feel trapped in this mood.

I take another drink of my whiskey. The buzzed feeling is working enough that I don't want it to stop. I don't want to leave this room, but I also can't hide in here forever. I clean my eyes up—though they are still red—and walk straight to the sofa. The fireplace is on and there is soft music coming from the speaker on the mantel. Sarah is still in the kitchen. I hear bags rattling around. Now I realize where she was this evening as she continues putting away groceries. I should probably go help her. Instead, I just sit where I am, sipping my caramel-flavored drink.

"Have you eaten?" Sarah asks. I can hear the difference in her voice now.

"Yes." I want to say more, but my mood is taking over. I honestly don't know if I've ever felt like this before. This is new territory.

"I made dinner tonight and saved you a plate. Just in case..." More bags rattle, the refrigerator opens then closes. "I'm going to shower," she says, walking past me and out of the room without ever looking my way.

This uncomfortable feeling is all my fault. I caused the tension between us. Sarah has been welcoming and considerate. It would be nice to snap out of this.

I hear the shower turn on. The sound of music fills the room, so I try to focus on that. The soft glow of the fireplace lights the otherwise dark room. I abandon my whiskey and grab a blanket from the back of the couch. I lie down with my back toward to the room and snuggle under the soft plush. I squeeze my eyes closed, trying to stop the tears from leaking out. I lose that battle.

Ten, fifteen, maybe twenty minutes pass before I hear Sarah's footsteps enter the room. I'm not sure how long it actually has been. I keep my eyes closed, pretending I'm asleep. Her presence makes me feel less alone. But that feeling is fleeting as Sarah turns off the music, shuts down the fireplace, and goes back to the bedroom. I don't know what I expected from her. Maybe to ask if I am okay or if I am coming to bed? But she has no reason to do that after the way I treated her earlier. I could just get up and go get in bed with her. Let her fill this void I'm experiencing. That's what I want to do. Instead, I close my eyes and let the darkness envelop me.

CHAPTER TWENTY-ONE

There are a lot of cars to choose from. I've never shopped for a vehicle before. I walk around the parking lot looking through the windows of a few, trying to decide which one I like most. After work, I came straight here. It's time for me to take this step. I have to keep moving forward.

"Hi, there," says a guy in a pink polo shirt and khaki pants. "Anything I can help you find today?"

"How much for this one?" I walk up to the black Jeep Wrangler that caught my eye. "And how many miles?" I peer through the window.

The car salesman leaves me behind while he runs back inside to get the keys. He returns to allow me to look inside. He lifts up the hood to show me the engine. I pretend to know what he's talking about. Then we go for a test drive. It's a 2008 model. I love it.

The salesman, Bruce, takes me inside the dealership to discuss the price. Even though I've never done this before, I know not to pay asking price. We go back and forth for some time before settling on a number. It would have been nice to have someone show me the ropes. But I think I do okay. I walk out with the keys to my first vehicle. I know exactly who I will tell first.

I slide into the driver's seat of my new old ride and run my hands over the steering wheel. It's a great feeling to have this new possession. I put the gear in drive and make excellent time over to the school. It makes me think about Sarah. She was gone before I woke from my spot on the sofa. It took me a few hours to actually fall asleep. When I realized she had left without a goodbye or *see you later* this morning, my chest felt tight with the hurt. I'm not sure how to handle things today with her. I'm feeling more like myself than last night, though my heart is still on the mend.

I pull into the parking lot of the school and park toward the back. The pavilion is straight ahead of where Brayden usually comes out. I decide to stand there and wait so I can see his face when he notices me. I've missed the boys. I'm excited to see them.

The bells rings, loudly dismissing school. Kids rush out the double doors, heading toward the car pickup line. Brayden is a bus rider, so he'll be out on the next bell. Or so I thought. He walks out the double doors with Mom. When he spots me, he instantly drops her hand and runs to me. His face is priceless.

"Bryn!" he says, the smile on his face is huge. I fill with joy from just that smile. He jumps into my arms, and I twirl him one time, enjoying the comfort he gives me.

"Hey, little man." I almost feel like crying from happiness. "How are you doing?"

"I missed you so much," he says. I lower him to the ground. "Can you come home now?"

Mom walks up to us and stands a couple feet away. I wonder why she is here today, but I'm not going to ask. She'll probably say it's none of my business.

"I have to get the rest of my things from the house. I wanted to see if you and Ben wanted to ride with me. I have something to show you." I look up at Mom, asking for permission without saying the words.

"Please, Mom. Can we go with Bryn?" I'm glad he chimed in. She's not my biggest fan. As I have learned.

"How can they ride with you? Did you borrow a car?" Mom looks awkward standing there looking at us. I've never seen her like this before.

"I bought a vehicle. I thought the boys would like a ride and maybe an ice cream on the way." I look at Brayden and wink.

"Yes!" Brayden jumps up and down. "Please, Mom. Please!"

Mom's upper lip curls in disdain. "Stop jumping around." She looks at me. "No ice cream. Just bring them straight home. We have dinner plans with Stan." She walks off, leaving me and Brayden staring at her back. But neither of us seem to care.

Brayden wraps his arms around me again. "I wish I could stay with you tonight."

"Maybe soon." I guide him toward the sidewalk with my hand on his shoulder so we can get Ben. "What was Mom doing here today? Are you having trouble at school again?"

"No." He shakes his head. "She wants to move me from Ms. Cain's class. But I don't want to move. I like Ms. Cain."

"Why does she want to move you?" Now I'm worried about Sarah. I don't want anything to happen with her job.

Brayden shrugs. "Don't know."

Shit. Another thing to be stressed about. Why does Mom have to be like this? And why can't I call her Brenda? It's not like she wants to be my mom anyway.

"Ben!" Brayden waves both arms in the air. "Over here." I'm sure he's going to be embarrassed by that. When he looks our way, I see that I'm wrong. He immediately jogs toward us, leaving his friends behind. He embraces me, wrapping his arms around my waist. I'm so surprised that I just hug him back. He hasn't hugged me in front of his friends in a long time.

"I'm happy to see you too, kiddo." I sway us side to side.

"Mom took our phones and said to leave you alone for a little while. I wanted to call you, Bryn. She wouldn't let me." Ben releases his grip and steps back. "Are you okay?" He looks at my bruised eye.

"I'm doing good," I lie. "Is everything okay at home? Did Stan move in yet?" I motion them to walk with me down the sidewalk and back toward where I parked.

"Yeah, he did. It's weird without you there. Mom hasn't been the same either. She's been…" Ben looks at me hesitantly. "Nicer." His eyes find the ground as if embarrassed to say it. My heart sinks a little. I still had some semblance of hope that she may love me like her own, and not the burden she considers me.

"I'm glad she is being good to you both. She loves you and Brayden." I put my arms around each of them as we walk, just needing the connection.

"I want you to come home," Brayden says. His eyebrows turn inward and his forehead creases.

"You know I can't do that. But maybe we can go somewhere this weekend and spend some time together. What do you say?" I look from Brayden to Ben.

"Sure." Ben nods. Brayden stays silent. He is upset, but he'll come around eventually.

We stop next to my black two-door Jeep. "Here it is." I throw my arms out to the side and smile widely.

"No fricking way!" Ben looks at me. "Is this yours for real?" He walks around to the front, then to the back. He runs his hand over the door.

"Got it today." I jiggle the keys. I decide to let his choice of word slide.

"Can we take the top off?" Brayden climbs up onto the sidestep and looks at the roof. "It comes off, right here, Bryn. Look."

I laugh, knowing this information already. But it's a hard top, so a little different taking off the whole thing than a convertible. "Not today, because I have nowhere to store it. But definitely next time if it's warm enough." I unlock the doors for the boys. They excitedly jump in, Brayden climbing into the back and Ben sitting up front next to me.

"This is so cool." Ben puts his books between his legs so he can buckle in.

I smile, feeling the best I have in a couple days. These guys have my heart. Always will. We roll down the windows, turn up the music, and the three of us sing the Darius Rucker song "Wagon Wheel" while we cruise down the highway. We are having a good time, but it ends way too soon, as I park on the street in front of the house.

"Are you coming in?" Ben says.

I turn the engine off. "Yeah. I need to grab the rest of my things." I get out and lift the seat for Brayden. We all walk up together. I feel nervous. Not sure why. But I do. I still have a key to the house, but I don't use it. The boys enter first. I follow and close the door behind us. Mom and Stan are sitting on the sofa.

"I'm just going to grab the rest of my things." I look toward them. "It won't take long."

Stan gets up with a grunt and walks toward me. "We moved all your things out of your room so I could use it as an office." He walks past me to the kitchen. When he returns, he hands me a key. "All of your stuff is in the storage room off the carport."

They certainly didn't waste any time—or give me time to do anything. I'm annoyed that they boxed up my belongings and put them out of the house. "Boys, want to help me carry my stuff to the Jeep?"

"Yeah, we'll help," Ben answers for them both. He taps Brayden on the shoulder before putting his books on the table. Brayden drops his backpack on the ground where he stands.

I open the storage door and look around. Boxes might have been good for my things. Instead, all my possessions are in trash bags. I push down my irritation. Ben and I grab two bags each. Brayden carries one. We stuff them in the Jeep. There isn't much room left in my compact vehicle. I go back in for the last bag, but first I need to talk to Brenda. She is still on the couch with Stan. The boys stand next to me, not leaving my side.

"I was wondering if I could get the boys on Saturday for a few hours or so?"

She looks over at me for the first time since walking in. "I'll think about it and let you know."

"Okay." I don't press her about it. I'm sure the boys will do that for me. She has never really told me no before when

I wanted to take them somewhere. She must be doing this for control. I turn to the boys. "Walk me out." I head toward the carport, grab my last trash bag, and stop at the end of the driveway. Brayden is fidgeting. Ben has his hands stuffed inside the pockets of his jeans.

"I'm sorry I didn't tell you they moved your stuff out." Ben looks distressed.

"Hey," I say, pulling him to my side and wrapping my arm around his shoulder. "It's not a big deal. It saved me the trouble."

"I just wish things were different." Ben looks up at me. I can tell this has hurt him. "We miss you."

"Yeah, Bryn. Please come back. You can share our room." Brayden sounds so optimistic that I don't want to crush him by telling him I'll never be back.

"Look, guys." I look from Ben to Brayden. "The only difference is that I'm not sleeping here anymore. I'll still come see you. If you want, I can pick you up from school and drive you home a few times a week. I'm sure Mom will be okay with that." I hope she will be, anyway. "This is all new for me too. But we will be okay. I'm always just a phone call away."

Brayden's lip quivers. "But it's not the same. Who will help me with my homework? Or take me to Uncle Ira's for a burger? Mom can't pick out my clothes."

"Brayden." I take hold of his hand. "I can still do all those things. You can call me for homework, or we can Facetime. Uncle Ira's is my, your, and Ben's place. We are still going to eat there together. And, of course, you are my best shopping pal. Two peas in a pod, you and I are." I hug him. "I love you."

"I love you too." He sniffles.

I stand up and pull Ben to me. "I love you, Ben. Take care of our little brother."

"I will. Love you too," he says.

I throw the last bag over into the front seat then wave bye as I pull out onto the road. I try not to think about how sad they are. Or how things are changing. That's just a part of life. We all move on whether it is a planned move or forced upon us. I'm not forgetting the past. I'm just accepting a different future. A better future, I hope.

CHAPTER TWENTY-TWO

It's dark by the time I get to Sarah's house. There is a car in the driveway as I pull up. I'm not sure who it could be. I park on the street across the road and wait. It's weird having my own transportation now. It gives me a sense of security.

I've thought about Sarah all day. She hasn't reached out to me. But neither have I. It's not because I didn't want to. I just didn't know what to say besides how sorry I am. Guess I could have started there.

I'm not sure if I should go in or not. I don't want to interrupt whatever is happening in there. I think I'll just wait until they leave. I went to class tonight, so I have plenty to keep me busy. Damon was there. I was nervous about seeing him, but thankfully we talked through it and moved on. I told him I'm with Sarah now. He said that after we left, he started connecting the dots. He apologized so many times about his behavior. It was nice that things went smoothly between us. With everything going on in my life, it's one less thing I have to worry about.

About twenty minutes later, I glance up to see someone walk out of Sarah's house. It's Ginny. I watch her walk down the walkway to her car. I wait until she is out of the driveway and on her way before I pull up to the garage.

The kitchen light is on when I enter the house. I hear the television when I get farther inside. Sarah is cleaning up. She looks up at me, surprise on her face but not in a good way. She continues to wipe down the counters without a word.

"Hi," I say, feeling awkward.

"Hey." She is most definitely upset. She scrubs around the top of the sink, putting a little more effort into it. "I didn't know if you'd be back tonight."

"Oh." I'm confused as to why she would think that. "I had class."

Sarah gives a brief nod. I would have missed it if I hadn't been paying attention. She drops the sponge in the sink, refills her wine, then walks out of the kitchen toward the bedroom. "I'm going to shower," she calls out over her shoulder, never looking back. I'm left standing there bewildered by what just transpired. I can assume many things have contributed to this reaction. For instance, me sleeping on the couch last night, or not speaking to her all day today. Maybe Mom going to the school. Whatever it is, I need to fix it.

The door to the bedroom is open when I get to the entry. So is the bathroom. "Sarah," I say softly, walking in and sitting on the side of the tub. I don't look at her naked body in the shower, though I very much want to. I respect her privacy. Also, I don't need to get distracted from my course of action.

"Yeah?" Her tone isn't harsh, just questioning.

"I apologize for being distant. I've had a tough couple of days, but that's no excuse. You have been thoughtful and giving. You deserve better than that." I look down at my feet, waiting for her response.

It feels like forever before she says anything back. "I understand," she says plainly. "When I get out, we should talk, though."

"Okay." I take that as my cue to leave. I find the jeans I wore yesterday and search the back pocket for the letter that changed my life.

A glass of whiskey is calling my name. I pour a glass with the ginger ale and head out to the patio. I take the top off the front of the firepit and turn on the gas. The rocks glow as the fire burns. I sit on the couch and pull the blanket over my lap for added warmth. The drink is sweet as I sip from the small glass.

Funny how Brenda is not my mother, yet I prefer whiskey like she does. I always wondered why I look nothing like her. I just assumed I got all those looks from Dad's side of the family, though I have no clue what he looks like. I've never seen a picture of him. If I ever asked what he was like, Mom would say he was a worthless piece of shit who didn't deserve to have his name on our lips. And now the thought that I had a mother I never knew is so unreal to me. What did this woman look like? Did she want me? I suppose I will never know.

It's not long before my thoughts are interrupted by the patio door opening. Sarah walks out carrying a full glass of wine. She is wearing a large cream-colored cardigan over a Norah Jones T-shirt, black fleece pants, and black socks. She looks comfortable. Her blond hair is a little damp from the shower and is in its natural wavy form. Her face is free of all makeup except for what looks like some sort of lotion. She is beautiful. Sliding onto the couch next to me, Sarah lifts her feet up under her. I offer part of my blanket and she accepts. She takes a drink of her wine and holds it close to her. She and Ginny were drinking earlier, if the two bottles on the bar when I walked in are any indication.

"I'm a little confused, Brynlee." Sarah looks at me, causing my heart to beat faster. "Have I done something wrong or made you uncomfortable in any way?"

"No." I shake my head. "Not at all."

"Then please tell me what's going on. You gave me the cold shoulder last night and then slept on the couch. That hurt. I thought I had a good idea of the kind of person you are, but…" She trails off, and so do her eyes. She stares into the burning flame as it dances across the glass rocks and takes another sip of her wine.

"Sarah, I am so sorry. It's all me. Not you." I feel awful for hurting her. She looks vulnerable and heartbroken.

She bobs her head a little. "Your mom showed up at the school today. She told lies to the principal about me, saying that Brayden was not learning in my class. That all the trouble he has had was due to me. She asked for him to be moved to another classroom. The principal wouldn't tell me everything she said, but it has bothered me terribly. I've tried to help Brayden and be there for him." Sarah sighs as she places her wine on the table. "He is looking into it. He told her that it's a little late in the year to make such a change."

"Mom is ridiculous," I say honestly. "I know Brayden loves you. You've been so helpful and caring. We are lucky to have you."

"I don't know, Brynlee." Sarah exhales a slow breath. "I'm feeling confused about so many things. One minute you seem like you want me, the next you don't seem to want me around. I'm not sure what to do because, honestly, you have stolen my heart. I didn't plan on this, but it happened. This back-and-forth is a little hard to take. And now this with work…" She sounds like she is on the brink of tears. I can't let her think I don't have feelings for her.

"Sarah." I take her hand. "I want you more than anything I've ever wanted in my life. I am sorry for pushing you away last night. I'm not sure I deserve you. I don't feel like I have much to offer." I look down at our hands. They fit perfectly together. "I'm going to explain my actions yesterday, but first I want to tell you something. Something that is hard for me to say. Something I have never told anyone ever." I look into her beautiful blue eyes. Eyes that express so much with one glance that sometimes they take my breath away. "I've fallen in love with you. I know it's quick. But I don't think there is a timeline on when it happens. I want you, and I want to be here. That is, if you will still give us a chance. I can do better."

Sarah's eyes get watery. She moves into my body, wrapping her arms around my neck. We hold each other, neither of us saying anything. Sarah is so close I can feel her heart pounding against me. I've missed this contact with her. She has such a good heart that all it took was me opening up for her to forgive me.

"I should have let you know what was happening," I whisper against her ear. "I'm usually not so selfish."

"I don't think you're selfish." Sarah pulls back to look me in the eyes. "Now that I know how you feel, it'll be easier to reach out. I thought about you all day."

"I thought about you too, but if you didn't already know how I feel, then I'm doing something wrong." I shrug.

"I'm sorry too," Sarah says. "I know this is not ideal circumstances to start a relationship in, and I just felt insecure after last night."

"And that's my fault." I gather my thoughts as I think about what I will say next. It's hard, but I need to keep going until she understands it all. "Yesterday, after lunch with Andrea, I went to the park for a while. I needed to be alone for this." I lift up the letter for her to see. "I was nervous about reading it, and for good reason."

"What is it?" Sarah looks at the paper in my hand with confusion.

"Here." I push it forward. "I want you to read it. Maybe I won't feel so alone if you do."

"Are you sure?" Sarah says. I nod. She takes the letter from my hand. I watch as she unfolds it and begins reading the words on the page. Her facial expression changes as she reads. She glances over at me briefly, eyes wide, then keeps reading. I can imagine the part she just read. I prop the side of my head against the couch but keep my eyes on Sarah. Her hand lifts to rest on her chest as she lowers the letter. "Brynlee," she says, shaking her head. "I'm so sorry, honey. I wish you would have told me this last night so I could have been there for you." She lifts her arm and I immediately lean into her, resting my head underneath her chin. She holds me close against her body. It's comforting.

"I just can't believe it," I say, trying to hold myself together.

"This is hard for anyone to wrap their head around." Sarah sighs. "My heart hurts for you. You've been through so much."

"Ben and Brayden will always be my brothers," I say softly, refusing to cry anymore.

"Of course. They love you, sweetheart. That is the undeniable truth." Sarah kisses the side of my head.

"I still don't understand why she would hurt me physically or talk down to me. I was a baby when I was dumped on her. I had no choice." The pain in my chest is tight. I feel the lump in my throat growing. I swallow it down.

Sarah squeezes me a little tighter. "I know, sweetheart. But at least you got Brayden and Ben out of it."

"I did. I do think that things happen for a reason. The boys needed me and I'm grateful I was there to help take care of them." It does help to think of it that way. Still, I have this void inside me. I believe it's always been there. Maybe some part of me has known all along that she has never loved me. "Why didn't my dad want me?" It's the one thought I've had over and over since reading the letter. "And why did Brenda hate me so much? I tried, Sarah." My voice sounds foreign to my ears as my tone lowers. "I wanted her to love me."

"Oh, baby." She puts her fingers under my chin, lifting my face. Her eyelashes are wet with tears. "I wish I knew the answers for you. But I can honestly say it's their loss. You are a wonderful person. You have a good heart. And I, for one, am so lucky to get to be a part of your life. You said earlier you didn't think you had much to offer me, but you do. You have so much more to offer than people with all the riches in the world."

Those words hit me hard. I've never had someone to make me feel so important before. I'm going to take this feeling and hold it close. I squeeze the arms that are wrapped around me, feeling warm in her embrace. "You are a bright star in my dark world."

I press my lips to Sarah's, feeling the need for the connection. I breathe her in, taking strength from her affection. When the kiss breaks, I stand and offer my hand to Sarah. I lead her inside, down the hall, and into the bedroom.

We make love slowly and passionately. I put everything I have into showing her how much she means to me. When we are sated and exhausted, we lie facing each other on our sides.

Sarah pushes my hair from my eyes, then lightly runs her fingertips over my mouth. "I love your lips," she whispers.

I kiss her finger before she takes it away. "And I love you," I confess. My heart pounds against my chest with the words I've never spoken to another woman before.

Sarah smiles, then reaches out to wipe a tear that has fallen down my cheek. "I love you too, baby." She sighs. "More than you know."

I move into Sarah's arms, where I feel safe. I have a lot to look forward to with this woman who makes my heart flutter, my thoughts happier, and my life fuller.

CHAPTER TWENTY-THREE

All week has been wonderful with Sarah. I come home from work and straighten up the house, then leave for night class. Sarah is home when I get back, with dinner ready. I've been having a glass of wine with her on occasion, forgoing the whiskey for personal reasons. Then we talk about our day. If I don't have work to finish for class, we shower together. And afterward we either watch television together while cuddling on the couch or turn in early to make love. It's been pretty great. All the feelings I have for Sarah prior to this week have amplified even more. I didn't realize that was possible. We have been in sync with each other without any disagreements.

Today is the topping of my amazing week. I've been looking forward to seeing the boys since I dropped them off on Monday. We did a video chat on Wednesday so they could tell me they could spend the day with me today. I haven't told them about Sarah yet. I'm going to do that today. Sarah has been the best. She has helped me plan the day and is excited to be included. I can't believe how lucky I am to have found her. The only thing about today that causes me a little unease is that I am going to talk to the boys about everything. Sarah and I agreed that it's best coming from me since Mom is so harsh with how she handles things. But first we are going to have fun.

"Are you ready for this, babe?" Sarah wraps her arms around my waist as I look in the mirror one last time. Her terms of endearment really get me in the feels. One of the many things I love about her.

"I am." I turn in her arms. "Thank you for being you."

The corners of her mouth lift upward. "Thank you for being *you*," she says back. "I think we are a great pair." She kisses me with those incredibly soft lips.

We walk to the door together. But I am going alone to get the boys. It still feels weird to have my own vehicle. I love my Jeep. Sarah had me drive her around the morning after I got it. We went for breakfast, then shopped for groceries together. I pushed the cart while she checked off the items on her list. And when we got home, she helped me organize my bags and put all my things away.

I put the Jeep in drive and wave to Sarah, who is still standing at the door. I will make a pit stop back for her later. I don't know why I'm so nervous right now. My hands feel shaky as I grip the steering wheel.

When I finally pull up in front of the house, the boys are standing on the stoop waiting. They stay put until I park next to the curb before bolting out toward me.

Ben opens the passenger-side door. "I still can't believe you have a ride." He smiles broadly as he lifts the seat for Brayden to climb in. "I want you to teach me to drive this." He shuts the door and buckles his seat belt.

"You have a few more years, bud. But I am definitely up to the challenge." I put the Jeep in drive and pull out. "How are you doing back there, little man?" I look in the rearview mirror at Brayden.

"Good," Brayden says, then gives me the silliest cheese smile. "What are we doing first?"

"I thought we'd go eat at Uncle Ira's for lunch. What do you think?"

"Yes!" both boys say in unison. I know it's their favorite place to eat.

"Glad you agree." I laugh. I think about Sarah's plan for today. She wanted me to spend time with the boys at lunch before she tagged along. I should have insisted she come with us. But I get why she wants me to have this time alone with them.

Uncle Ira's is usually always busy on Saturdays. Luckily, we are going to beat the lunch crowd. The boys jump out of the Jeep. I follow them inside and then over to our usual booth in front of the window.

We all order almost the exact same of hamburgers, fries, and sodas. Ben is sitting across from me and Brayden is beside me, next to the window.

"So, guys," I start. My anxiety starts creeping in. "I have a place I've been staying this week. It's with someone special I am in a relationship with."

"Who is it?" Brayden looks up at me.

"Well, actually you know her. It's Ms. Cain." I smile. "Sarah." I wait to see if they are shocked by my confession or maybe have questions about it being a woman. I've never told them I date women before.

"I love Ms. Cain!" Brayden claps his hands together. "Is she coming to eat with us?"

"No. But we are going to get her after we eat so she can meet Ben properly." I look at Ben. He hasn't said anything yet. "How do you feel about this?" I ask him.

He shrugs. "I kind of knew."

I chuckle at his confession. "How?"

"When you were texting and then went outside to talk. You were acting all…" He wraps his arms around himself to touch his back, then rubs his hands all around then up and down like he is caressing someone, all while he makes kissy faces.

"Stop." I laugh. Ben and Brayden join in.

The rest of lunch is fun. The boys don't talk about Mom, which I prefer. They tell me about their week and how much they miss me. My heart is full thinking of how easily they have accepted who I love. I may have been dealt a crappy hand, but having these two has made all the difference for me. I'm thankful beyond question for them.

After lunch I drive us back to Sarah's. The boys are quiet on the ride over. So am I. I pull into the driveway earlier than expected. "Want to take part of the roof off?" I look at the boys.

"Yes!" they both practically shout. I open the garage on the right side. Sarah gave me an opener and told me to park there. I don't pull in, but we will need to store the two pieces inside the garage.

"Okay. But I need both of you to help." I smile, knowing they love when I involve them in the things I do.

We work on unscrewing the inside first. I direct the boys on what to do. It's pretty simple. We have the first piece almost off when Sarah comes out to greet us. I stop and climb down.

"Ben, Brayden." I motion for them to come over. "This is Sarah. My girlfriend." I look at her and smile. This is the first time I've introduced her that way.

"It's nice to see you again, Brayden." Sarah playfully winks at him, and he giggles. "Ben." She holds out her hand. "I've heard very good things about you from these two."

Ben shakes her hand. I can see a hint of pink tinting his cheeks.

"We are taking off part of the roof." I motion toward the Jeep. "Want to help?"

"Oh, you guys look like you've got it handled."

I climb back up and lift the driver-side panel. "Ben, come over here."

Ben scurries up to my side. I gently lower the panel to him. "Where do I put it?" he asks, taking it carefully from my hands.

"I'll show you." Sarah leads Ben into the garage.

I go around to the passenger side and lift the last panel up and off.

"Want me to get it?" Brayden says, his little arms raised in the air.

"It's heavy, little man. How about we lower it together?" I let him take one end of it as I climb down holding most of the weight. "You got your end?" He nods. "Okay let's carry it to the garage."

It's a beautiful day. I couldn't ask for a better afternoon to spend with the boys. It's a little chilly, but it's warmer than it has been over the last few weeks. I feel like it was meant just for us.

Sarah and Ben take the panel from us and place it in the garage. "Now that's some teamwork," Sarah says.

"Where are we going?" Ben asks.

I look at Sarah. "How about some indoor fun at the arcade?" I know how much the boys love doing that. "And maybe we can bowl afterward."

"Yay!" Brayden throws a fist in the air.

"Can you come, Sarah?" Ben asks.

"I'd love to," Sarah says, a smile spreading across her face.

* * *

It's almost dinner time when we get back to Sarah's. Or maybe I should start saying "our place," since I officially live here. Everything is still so new that it will take some getting used to.

We had the best time today. Ben and Brayden played in the arcade for a long while. Sarah and I followed them around, cheering them on. Occasionally, Sarah and I played a game against each other or the boys. Then we bowled. I'm happy to say that I won with Ben coming in closer than I thought he would. Brayden and Sarah gave it their best and never gave up.

The plan now is to make the boys dinner since they don't have to be home until after. They wanted either spaghetti or pizza. Sarah went with spaghetti and has shooed us off to the living room with a game while she gets everything ready. Ben, Brayden, and I are sitting at the coffee table in the living room where I have Jenga set up.

"Who's first?" Ben asks, rubbing his fingers together like he is itching to get started.

"Um…" I look for the directions. It's been forever since I've played.

"Me! Pleaseee," Brayden begs.

I look at Ben. "Go ahead," he says sarcastically. I laugh.

As the game begins, we each take a turn pulling out a block. I'm working up the nerve to talk to them about Brenda. Sarah is cooking in the kitchen, and I know she can hear us, though she is busy doing her own thing.

"So, boys," I say, easing out a block slowly. "I need to tell you something important. Please keep an open mind."

"Are you and Sarah getting married?" Brayden blurts out.

"Brayden." I laugh, nervously. And I can hear Sarah chuckle from the kitchen.

"That would be pretty cool," Ben says, almost nonchalant. Obviously, he approves of Sarah.

I shake my head and catch a glimpse of Sarah at the sink. She winks at me. "Thanks, boys. I'm glad you approve of Sarah. She is a keeper."

Ben taps on a block to get it started. It wobbles a little, but he is able to pull it out slowly. "So, what is it?" he says, placing the block on top of the stack. "What's the big news?"

I have a moment of nervousness so overwhelming that I feel sick. Sarah must notice, because the next thing I know she is squatted next to me, her hand on my back.

"Brynlee," she says softly. "Honey, it's okay."

Something clicks when I hear her voice. I turn to look into the comforting sea of blue that is her eyes. I take a deep breath, realizing that I straight-up had an anxiety attack. My first ever. I take her hand in mine and hold it, willing her to stay next to me for strength as I tell the boys the truth that I wish weren't so. She sits next to me on the floor, pulling my hand into her lap and squeezing it to let me know she is with me. I look at the boys, who seem upset by my actions. They have never seen me like this before.

"Hey, guys." My voice breaks. I hate being like this. I thought I was stronger than this. "I'm okay. I promise. I just…well, I want you both to know that I love you with all my heart. Now and forever. Okay?" They nod even though I can tell they are confused and upset. I'm not helping the situation whatsoever with my emotions. "Remember when Mom got upset with me at the house last week?"

"You mean when she punched you?" Ben corrects.

I nod, not wanting to say it like that. "Well, when I was leaving that day, she handed me a letter." I exhale a breath, and Sarah holds my hand a little tighter. "In that letter, she told me that when I was a little baby, just a newborn, she met my dad and fell in love. My biological mother died giving birth to me. So, when my dad met your mom, Brenda, she agreed to take care of me." I'm not about to tell them all that Brenda said or that she didn't want to be burdened by me. I would never put them in a position to feel hurt toward their mom.

"I'm confused," Brayden says.

"Bryn doesn't have the same mom as us," Ben tells Brayden. "But she is still our sister." He looks right at me. "Blood doesn't make us family."

"Love does," I finish. "We may not share genetics, but I have been there since the day you were born. I wiped your noses, picked you up when you fell, and held you when you cried. You are my family forever. My sweet handsome little brothers."

Brayden gets up and comes over to me. He climbs in my lap, wrapping his little arms around my neck and resting his head on my shoulder. Ben comes over to the opposite side of Sarah and squats down next to me, enveloping both Brayden and me with his long arms. Sarah joins in from her side for one big hug. I realize it's not the moments in life that tear our heart open that define us. It's the ones that mend us back together. The ones that show us what life is worth. I have my whole world in this embrace. I'm pretty lucky.

CHAPTER TWENTY-FOUR

It's graduation day. The months have flown by and I still can't believe it's here. My life has changed so much within this time, and for the better. I have my degree that I worked hard for, and on Monday morning, courtesy of my teacher for being the top student, I have an interview with a very prestigious company. I can honestly say that for the first time in my life I'm completely happy. My anxiety levels have dropped dramatically since moving in with Sarah. It's amazing how one person can impact someone's life so much. I'm here to tell you it's true. True for both Sarah to the better, and Mom for the lesser effect. I haven't completely stopped calling Brenda "Mom" yet. To the boys I will always refer to her that way.

I look out over the crowd from my place on the stage. The ceremony has already begun, and I don't see Sarah anywhere. I drove myself because I had to be early, and she said she'd be here. I wouldn't think she would miss it, but I don't understand what has kept her. I locate Andrea and Aimee, who are waving wildly at me, big smiles on their faces. I wave back, happy to see two of my favorite people here to support me. As I'm waving to them. Andrea turns her head toward the aisle. My eyes move with her to find three perfect faces. Sarah, Ben, and Brayden are here. Sarah brought the boys! I called Brenda to ask if they could come last week, but she said no. They had plans. But here they are with Sarah. I can't believe it. I really wanted them to be a part of this special day. I don't know how she managed it, but I do believe she is completely amazing.

Sarah and the boys slide into the seats next to Andrea and Aimee. Ben and Brayden wave at me. I wave back. I catch Sarah's gaze, who is sitting between the boys, and my heart swells with love for her. She blows me a kiss, which makes my cheeks heat. I don't mind at all. Hell, I would shout it for the world to know—if the world cared.

"Brynlee Anne McAdams." My name is called.

I walk up to take my diploma, and as I shake the dean's hand, I turn toward the crowd. Sarah and Andrea have made their way in front to take a picture, both snapping away. I smile with true affection. This is my family. My true family. They are here to share a moment in life that will one day become a memory. A memory that I will look back on fondly.

* * *

"How's the grilling coming along?" Andrea bumps her shoulder against mine. She is holding a glass of wine that Sarah has poured.

"Almost ready," I say. After the ceremony, we all came back to the house to grill out. Sarah is inside putting together the sides to go with the hamburgers and hot dogs I have on the grill. The kids are sitting by the firepit playing Jenga.

"You seem so much lighter. And really happy." Andrea moves to the side of the grill so she can see me straight on. "Sarah is good for you."

"I agree to all those things." I look in through the glass doors to see Sarah mixing something in a bowl. She has admitted to me how much she loves cooking for everyone. I place the tongs on the hook of the grill. "I'm very lucky."

"So, when are you meeting the parents?" Andrea takes a sip of her wine. "Aimee," she calls out. "Do not stand over the fire like that. Sit your butt down please, ma'am."

I laugh. I'm used to Andrea stopping mid-sentence to say something to Aimee. I just roll with it now. "I'm meeting them next Friday night for dinner at Le Fleur's."

"Ohh…fancy!"

"Right?" I shrug. Le Fleur's is an upscale restaurant about thirty minutes away. "Also, Sarah's sister and her husband are coming. I'm not nervous at all." I go wide-eyed to prove my point.

Andrea laughs. "Want me to go as the buffer? You know I'll have them loving your little ass by the time dessert is ordered."

"Please." I chuckle. "More like before the entrées arrive."

"You know that's right!" She taps her wineglass to mine. "But for real, you seem so different now. I'm happy for you, bestie."

"Thanks." I smile. "I'm in the best place I have ever been."

Andrea unexpectedly puts her arm around my shoulders for a side hug. "You two are so damn cute, I can barely stand it."

I laugh. "She makes me look better."

"Please, girl. You know you got the right stuff."

I shake my head. "You know just how to boost my confidence."

"Well, it's true." Andrea looks over at the boys. "How's everything with Brenda?"

"It's not great. But I don't expect much from her anymore." Andrea had been shocked when I finally told her everything. I think she might have been a little hurt that I didn't come to her first, but she understood. She is one of those people you meet in life that just gets you. She knows when I need to be pushed, or when I need space. And most importantly, she is always there, no matter what. She is a true best friend.

"It's time to let that go. You tried. You were a good daughter. If she doesn't appreciate you, that's her loss. You have plenty of people who do."

"I know," I say. "It just hurts sometimes. She is the only mother I have ever had. I love her, I can't help it. I guess I just wish she loved me back." I flip the meat one last time, leaving the top up.

Andrea sighs loudly. "She is a selfish person, B. You have to find a way to shake it off. Not all mothers, biological or not, are good. This happens all the time to good people like you. And though it doesn't make it right or take away from what you feel, you have to know you did nothing wrong. This is not about you. It's about her."

"You're right." I nod. "Thanks for being my voice of reason."

"You know I've got you."

I take the food off the grill and we all head inside to eat. I think about what Andrea said and I know without a doubt she is right. I have to let go and move on. When I finally realized that Brayden wasn't the only one being bullied by someone, it hurt. My mother hurt me beyond reason, and I never thought of her as a bully. But that is what she was to me. Yet I find myself missing her on days. And I'm not sure if it's her I miss, or the idea of her.

While Andrea is helping the kids fix their plates, Sarah asks to see me in the foyer. She walks over to her jacket and pulls out a piece of paper.

"Brenda gave me this to give you. Apparently, your dad contacted her a few years ago trying to reach out to you. This is his address."

I take the folded piece of paper from Sarah's hand. I stare at it but do not open it. On the top is his name: Bryan Lee McAdams.

"I'll give you a minute alone. We'll wait on you." She touches my arm as she walks by.

My dad contacted Brenda and she didn't tell me. Not that he has any right to see me now. He missed my whole life. I'm tempted to open the paper to see what it says. Instead, I push it in my pocket and head to the kitchen. Everyone is at the table except for Sarah. She hands me a plate and has me fix my plate first. I take my food over to the dining room and join everyone else.

"You okay, baby?" Sarah asks, taking her seat next to me.

"Absolutely." I smile. "Thank you for all of this. You really have no idea how much it means to me."

Sarah reaches over and kisses me on the lips, quick and soft. "I love you more than words," she says. "So, yes, I do know how much it means."

My heart beats a little faster with her admission. This journey with Sarah has been just what I needed to show me what love is and that I can be truly happy. It's the first time in my life I have gone a whole week without someone talking down to me or making me feel insignificant. She makes me stronger just being around her.

I take the paper from my pocket that has my dad's information on it and rip it up so that Sarah can see. I take her hand and pull it into my lap. "I don't need to find him. He had his chance. I have my family right here at this table." I lean over and kiss her. "I love you."

The boys are smiling when I look over at them. I never asked Sarah how she managed to change Brenda's mind. Sarah loves me enough to fight for me. I feel it in her hugs, or the way she looks at me, and even the way she squeezes my hand a little tighter at exactly the moment when I need it the most. I believe people come into our lives at the right time. And though Sarah and I met under unfortunate circumstances with Brayden, I feel like it was meant to be. I look around the table at each of the smiling faces. I am lucky to be loved by each of them. These people are the pieces to my puzzle. I am complete.

Bella Books, Inc.

Women. Books. Even Better Together.

P.O. Box 10543
Tallahassee, FL 32302

Phone: 800-729-4992
www.bellabooks.com